James Barnes

The Hero of Erie

James Barnes

The Hero of Erie

ISBN/EAN: 9783337192075

Printed in Europe, USA, Canada, Australia, Japan

Cover: Foto ©Andreas Hilbeck / pixelio.de

More available books at **www.hansebooks.com**

THE HERO OF ERIE

(OLIVER HAZARD PERRY)

BY

JAMES BARNES

AUTHOR OF COMMODORE BAINBRIDGE,
MIDSHIPMAN FARRAGUT, NAVAL ACTIONS
OF THE WAR OF 1812, ETC.

ILLUSTRATED

NEW YORK

D. APPLETON AND COMPANY

1898

CONTENTS.

LIST OF FULL-PAGE ILLUSTRATIONS.

NOTE.—The publishers wish to acknowledge the courtesy of
Charles T. Harbeck, Esq., whose collection has supplied
the old engravings reproduced in this volume. The dia-
grams in the text are from *A History of the United States
Navy*, 1775-1898, by Edgar Stanton Maclay, A. M.

THE HERO OF ERIE.

CHAPTER I.

WHEREIN OLIVER LEARNS WHAT HIS FATHER DID.

CAPTAIN CHRISTOPHER RAYMOND PERRY had just returned home from a long voyage to the East Indies. It was the year 1795. Since his marriage, twelve years previously, he had been making long voyages, and spending but little time with his family. But this is what a sailor's family have to become used to. His comings and goings, like his life when afloat, were uncertain; sometimes months and months would go by without the eager ones at home receiving a word from the beloved parent or brother, and then suddenly his ship would come into port, and before word could be sent ahead of him he would drop into the home circle as suddenly as if he had descended from the skies.

Mrs. Perry had known that her husband was on the seas returning, and perhaps it was her prayers that gave the vessel fair winds and pleasant weather. A

sailor has a way of expressing this when on a home-
ward voyage; if everything is going finely, he says:
"The girls at home, sweethearts and wives, must have
hold of our towline." And many times had Captain
Perry made this observation to himself, for he had
sighted Block Island, bound into Providence, almost
a fortnight before he had expected to in the due
course of events. The moon rose early at this time
of the month, and in its bright rays he had crept past
Point Judith and the Island of Canonicut, and had
dropped his anchor before midnight well up the harbor. Mrs. Perry, who lived in the town of South
Kingston, had been awakened by a knocking on the
door, and, wondering what the message could be, had
gone down to open it. She had seen a figure standing there, and with a cry of joy she had found herself in her husband's arms. The children did not
know that a great, strong man, whose eyes had filled
with tears, had looked down upon them that night as
they lay asleep; but early in the morning the news
had spread about the house, the welcome, joyful
words, "Father has come home from sea!" When
they came down to breakfast they felt a little strange
and half frightened, for their parent's stay was never
long, and sometimes the tones of his voice, and even
his appearance, had almost faded from their minds.
Soon after the morning meal, which the young ones
ate in rather a constrained silence, Captain Perry had

to leave again to superintend the unloading of his
ship.

But the next day being Sunday, he spent it with
them, and late in the afternoon he had called to his
oldest boy, Oliver, and hand in hand they had walked
through the orchard and the lower meadow until they
had reached a place where two large maples threw a
grateful shade upon the grass.

Captain Perry seated himself, and leaned back
against the trunk of one of the trees and drew a long
breath of pure contentment. What man could be hap-
pier? He had finished a successful voyage. He had
found his family all alive and well. He was young, not
even yet in what people term "the prime of life." He
looked down at the peaceful river, and dropped his
head forward on his chest; far away he could just see
the masts of his vessel lying safe at anchor. He listened
to the humming of the bees and the murmur of the
insects, and to the gentle rustle of the leaves above
his head, and no wonder he felt contented. No wonder
he closed his eyes and drew again a thankful, heartfelt breath. Suddenly the little boy who had nestled
by his knee, and who had been rather shy at first, in-
terrupted his thoughts.

"Father," he said, looking up with great round
eyes into his parent's face, "tell me a story."

Now, to a man in a happy frame of mind there is
no such pleasant task as to tell stories to a young

and appreciative listener; and if the listener happens to be a child of his own, surely the pleasure is more than doubled, and the story can not fail to be of interest. There was evidence of that in the very attitude of this expectant audience of one. He had clasped both hands upon his parent's knee, and had rested his round chin upon them, and the father looked down on the boy's face and smiled. He felt inspiration growing within him. Some day perhaps this boy would be telling stories in his turn, and so he began:

"How old are you, Oliver, my son?"

"Ten my last birthday, father."

"Well, then, I'll begin when I was your age. I wasn't quite so tall as you are now, but I was very strong——"

"I'm not very strong," put in Oliver, in a sad, apologetic little tone.

"Never mind that, son," went on his father, "you've grown so fast; why, you're a half head taller than most boys of your age, and you'll grow up to your strength, too; and now I'll go on with the story: I lived here in the same house where you live now. I went to the schoolhouse that you go to, and old Mr. Judson, whom you often see in his big white wig and snuffy coat on the streets, was my schoolmaster. Things are very little changed; I could almost imagine, as I look about me, that I am your age again. These trees were not quite so tall as they are now, and

there are a few new houses on the hillside, and the
meeting-house has a new steeple, but, as I say, all is
about the same. I played the same games that
you do; I set traps for squirrels and woodchucks, and
I gathered birds' nests in the spring and chestnuts in
the fall, and fought snowball fights in the winter, and
so you know by looking around you what my life was,
and how happy a boy can be who has little care and
sorrow. But all this time every one was talking of
the troubles of the country, and saying that it would
be but a short time before we would be at war with
England. The talk increased every day, and the
troubles brewed, until one morning the news was
brought to us by the postboy that the country had risen
and that a battle had been fought, and that the war
was on. I was but fifteen years old when this took
place. I had sailed in boats on the river, as you do now
with your companions, and I had made one or two
little voyages out on the sound, and so I became filled
with the idea that I must be a sailor, and that the
country was in great need of my services as such.
For a long time my family would not hear of it—
imagine how your mother would hate to see you leave
her—but at last, when the war was on about a year,
I obtained their permission to leave home, and embarked as cabin boy on board a privateer commanded
by Captain Reed. The life of a sailor is a hard one
at the best; perhaps no man works harder and has

fewer comforts. He must be ready at all times to tumble out of his cozy hammock and go on the wet, slippery deck, or he must climb aloft in the cold, cutting snowstorm, to help furl sail. He must be ready to fight when called upon, and he must be obedient to orders, always alert and vigorous. As the old song goes, ' he must be all of one part with his ship.' Some lads take naturally to this sort of life, and perhaps without boasting I may say that I did. I thrived in the rough life, and when I returned after my first voyage my folks scarcely knew me, I had grown so brown and strong."

The boy, whose grasp had tightened on his father's knee, winced a little, and Captain Perry, who had not noticed this, once more drew a long breath, looked up to the peaceful branches of the tree above his head, and out once more on to the shimmering reaches of the river. He paused for a few minutes, and mayhap his thoughts wandered back more vividly to the stirring days of twenty years before. But the boy never took his eyes off his father's face. In his mind a firm resolve was growing. In that flash of time he decided for himself, as many a youngster has upon an instant decided his future and lived to round it out.

"Go on, father," he said quietly; "pray don't stop."

Captain Perry placed his hands on the boy's head, and took up his tale again. He went on to tell of how

he had volunteered upon the public vessel of war
Trumbull, and how he had fought on her until he
had gained command of one of the broadside guns,
and how, after this voyage he had volunteered on
board the sloop-of-war Mifflin, commanded by Captain
Babcock, and how he was taken prisoner when she
was captured by the enemy, and confined on board the
dreadful prison ship Jersey. He told of the horrible
sufferings; of the starvation and disease that carried
off the prisoners by the score; of how at one time a
boat would come twice a day to take away the dead.
He told how he had seen strong men waste away to
living skeletons and wish to die. When he came to
the part of his narrative in which he related how again
and again he planned to escape, and how at last the
dreadful prison fever laid hold of him, the boy began
to gasp, and the father paused, then hurried on the
telling. When he came to the part that told of his
liberation, little Oliver sighed with relief, and so the
tale proceeded. Captain Perry in graphic words described how he had again taken service on board a
private armed brig commanded by Captain Rathbone,
and had cruised on a voyage full of excitement, straight
into the English Channel. Here again he had been
taken prisoner, and for eighteen months was confined
in a British prison. When he related his thrilling
escape from this, Oliver was panting and almost trem-
bling with excitement. Closely he followed the rest of

the story—how his father had, after a life of vicissitude
in London, managed to ship aboard an English vessel
bound for the island of St. Thomas, whence he had
made his way to Charleston, South Carolina, and
there soon learned that peace had been declared. This
same year he had made a voyage to Scotland, and returned as mate of the vessel.

"And who do you suppose was on that voyage
with me, Oliver?" he asked.

"I know," the boy put in; "mother was. She
told us all about it once."

Captain Perry again drew a long breath. "She
was indeed, my son," he said. "It was there I met
her, and it was the luckiest voyage of all my life, and
the luckiest voyage I shall ever make."

It was so dark by this time that lights had begun
to twinkle in the windows of the farmhouses across
the river. The captain drew his great watch out of
his pocket. "Whew!" he whistled, imitating the boat-
swain's call, "pipe down all hands! Mother must be
wondering what has become of us. Come, my lad,
let's have a run back to the house. Ahead with you,
and see what your legs are good for." They struck
into a dog-trot, hand in hand, and every turn in
the path the captain would sing out, "Hard astar-
board now!" or "Hard aport!" as the case might
be, until at last they dropped anchor on the door-
step, and announced their arrival with a hail,

"Supper ahoy, there!" and a rush into the dining room.

Mrs. Perry was unpacking the box containing the wonderful East Indian shawls and some odds and ends of trinkets the captain always brought back with him from his voyages; and then Oliver boldly spoke out his thoughts: "Mother," said he, with his check against her shoulder, "some day I'm going to be a sailor"—he paused—"like father," he added.

"Then, Oliver," returned Mrs. Perry, glancing at her husband, "you will have to be a very good one."

Like every boy whose head is full of but one idea, the lad could dream of nothing that night but ships and the sea; and when the next day he accompanied his father down to the vessel he tried to imagine himself in command of her, and grew quite excited as his mind suggested fights and adventures.

CHAPTER II.

THE MIDSHIPMAN.

BEFORE Captain Perry had sailed away he had promised Oliver to do everything in his power to secure for him an appointment in the navy. The naval force at this time belonging to the United States was practically nothing. We possessed no first-class ship, and hardly a vessel in commission was kept in proper shape. There were a few gunboats in some of the ports, useless vessels, take it altogether, and the finances of the Naval Department were at low ebb. Oliver went to school at Newport. He had become a boy of but one idea. Maybe the love of the sea was in his blood, for such things are sometimes an inheritance. At all events, he dreamed of it and thought of it, and read all the books that he could possibly lay hand to that dealt with seafaring life. He would spend his spare hours along the water front, and with the assistance of an old sailor he began the construction of a miniature full-rigged ship.

Every time his father returned from his voyages during the next few years he found his son still growing, and still in the same settled purpose—that of fol-

lowing in his footsteps. And now a great change
took place in Captain Perry's life. Early in the year
1798 Captain Perry left the merchant service and
accepted the command of the United States frigate
General Greene, and upon his return from his first
cruise he secured the appointment so long wished
for, and returned home in April, 1799, for a short stay.
When he joined his ship, young Oliver Hazard Perry,
dressed in a new midshipman's uniform, was with him.
Some people might have considered it a drawback
for a lad to have commenced his career by serving in
the same vessel his father commanded, but Oliver was
a boy of too much individuality either to be hindered
by this connection or to take advantage of it. He
took his place among the other midshipmen naturally
and without assumption. He worked hard and dili-
gently at his studies, and soon became the leader in
the steerage so far as mathematics was concerned.
Now, if a boy supposes that by leaving school and
going to sea he is going to escape the drudgery of
study and the dry poring over dull facts and figures,
he is mistaken. All the work that he has done heretofore will be found to be nothing when compared with
that which he has to go through with in the service
—that is, of course, if he wishes to become an officer
and earn the attention and respect of superiors and
inferiors alike.

The General Greene had set sail at once for the

Havana station, and, in a short cruise of three months in those waters, convoyed more than fifty merchant vessels to different ports of the United States. She would probably have stayed longer had it not been that a contagious fever broke out in the forecastle, and she was ordered home to spend a long time in quarantine.

Midshipman Perry had now begun to grow up to his height, his muscles were becoming developed and hard, his shoulders and chest had broadened, and his face had become fuller; altogether he was a very different-looking lad before the end of the year was out, and all this his father noticed with satisfaction. Every morning before breakfast on board the General Greene the midshipmen were sent in a scamper up the shrouds to the maintop, and down again the other side, and this was twice repeated. Any one who might consider this light exercise had best try it for himself. It was not long before Midshipman Perry was a leader in this sport, as well as in the study of navigation and the languages.

Although Captain Perry saw no more of his son than he did of the other midshipmen, he was delighted and proud. He perceived that there was the making of an officer in his boy, and often his eye glistened when the junior officers spoke well of Oliver. As for the midshipman himself, his admiration and love for his father grew and expanded daily, and he be-

lieved firmly that with him in command nothing could
go wrong, no enemy would ever be able to take the
ship, no storm would battle her, no misfortune overcome her.

A little incident that occurred while the General
Greene was still cruising in the Gulf is well worth mentioning, because it shows so plainly the independence
and the boldness of spirit that the early Yankee captains seemed to possess. One bright day, while on a
voyage from New Orleans to Havana, with a large
merchant brig under convoy, a great sail well up to
windward was seen bearing down, and soon it was made
out that the stranger was a British seventy-four. The
brig was also to windward of the General Greene, and
thus the British battle ship approached her first. She
was a faster sailer than either of the American vessels,
and, although the words could not be heard, it was
evident to all on board the General Greene that the
stranger was hailing the brig, who edged off a little
without replying. Probably angered at being thus
ignored, the English captain fired a gun across the
smaller vessel's bows, but no attention was paid to this,
and both Yankee ships sailed on, minding their own
business and betraying not the least flurry of excitement. Quietly the crew of the frigate was called to
quarters, for it was made out that the Englishman was
up to some trickery. Forging ahead of the brig once
more, he dropped a boat without heaving to, and

an armed crew slipped down into her, but soon after
they had taken up their oars, and before they reached
the little vessel's side, Captain Perry had given a few
instructions to one of the gunners of the first division
on the spar deck to bring his piece to bear upon the
boat.

"Handsomely, now, my man," said Captain Perry,
"and see if you can make a good shot of it."

"Am I to try to hit her, sir?" asked the gunner,
a little astonished.

"If you can," answered the captain laconically.

What would have happened if that shot had struck
the small boat it might be hard to say; as it was, it
slammed into the water but a few feet astern of her,
and deluged the men in the stern sheets with a shower
of spray. The men at the oars apparently did not
like the idea of becoming a target, and stopped rowing.
Their boat drifted down with the wind until it reached
the side of the General Greene, but the seventy-four had
begun to act like a very angry mother hen whose one
chick had been disturbed and frightened. Her yards
swung around with a clatter, and bristling and bustling
she bore down upon the little frigate. Then she swung
about so as almost to blanket her, and an officer on
the quarter-deck of the Englishman appeared at the
rail, trumpet in hand, and hailed angrily:

"What ship is that?"

"The United States frigate General Greene."

"Why did you fire at my boat just now?"

"To prevent her boarding that brig. She is under my protection, sir."

The Englishman's irritated outburst in reply to this caused the officers on the General Greene's quarter-deck to smile, despite the rather serious aspect of affairs.

"It is a strange thing," roared the British captain, "if one of his Majesty's seventy-four-gun ships can not examine a merchant brig."

Captain Perry hailed back through his own trumpet a reply to this:

"If she carried one hundred and twenty guns she should not do it to the dishonor of my flag."

A consultation was held on the Englishman's decks, and then the captain came to the rail again.

"Pardon me for having been apparently hasty," he said, "but have you any objection to my boarding the brig?"

Captain Perry looked out across the water for an instant, and then responded in tones quite as polite:

"If her captain has no objections, I have none," he responded. "You had better ask him, sir."

"Thank you, sir," answered the British captain.

"Good-day to you, sir."

"Good-day, sir."

And now the Yankee officers could not keep from

laughing. During all this talk the little brig had been making short tacks and beating up into the wind, until she had so well gained the weather gauge that it would take the Englishman full half a day, despite his speed, to be on even terms again. As soon as he had perceived what had happened, as if deciding that the game was not worth the candle, he gave it up, and bore away to the southward before the wind. Very soon the brig and the frigate joined company again, and without any further adventures they reached their destination.

In the year 1800, with the same officers and the same crew, the General Greene was dispatched to cruise in the waters surrounding the island of Haiti, and here the midshipmen had an opportunity to see a little fighting, for off the port of Jacmel the General Greene dropped anchor. The inhabitants of the island were then in revolt, and were under the leadership of the celebrated negro general, Toussaint l'Ouverture. As the United States had for some years been upon bad terms with France, and as the independence of the island was considered to be more promising to American commerce, the General Greene assisted in the reduction of the fort, and after blockading the port for some time she joined with her batteries in an engagement which resulted in the evacuation of the town by the enemy, and the surrender of the fortress and garrison eventually.

The General Greene suffered but little in the action, and no lives were lost.

Oliver and his father did not part until the following year, 1801, when the naval force of the nation was reduced again to almost nothing. In the fall of this year the corsairs of Tripoli commenced such depredations upon American commerce that it was deemed necessary to send three frigates and a sloop of war to the Mediterranean at once. Young Perry was attached to the Adams frigate, under the command of Captain Campbell. So successful was this little fleet that the pirates were driven practically from the Mediterranean waters to the protection of their ports, and thousands upon thousands of dollars were saved to American commerce.

In 1803 Perry returned to the United States. He was now an acting lieutenant at the age of eighteen, but age counted little in these days when the country itself was young. Experience, coolness of judgment, and bravery were qualifications that offset those of extreme youth. It was the era of young men—young men in politics, young men in business life, and young men in the service of their country, who builded its glories and successes into a monument of the times emblazoned with the records of brave deeds not to be forgotten while the nation is a nation, and the flag they fought for floats above us. It might be well to try to understand the reasons why young men should

be placed in such responsible positions as they filled
in the early part of this century. In the first place,
the lack of education among the lower classes of the
people, from which were drawn the ordinary sailor
before the mast, was a great drawback to advancement
of men from the ranks. Probably the majority of
them could read and write, but a youth whose preparation for service at sea embraced the study of mathematics and navigation, enabling him to work a vessel's
course, and determine latitude and longitude by the
sun or any of the heavenly bodies, soon found himself at the head of men whose experience afloat might
equal the sum of his entire life. The early experience of
the midshipmen was of the most practical kind, and
the officer of a ship, besides being a navigator, must
perforce be able to understand and perform the duties
of the commonest sailor. Thus he gained their respect, and they knew that they could trust him; for,
with all his knowledge of things they did not understand, he regarded things from their point of view also.

But to return to our hero. In 1804 we find him,
then, in the Mediterranean under the same commander
as before, and on board one of the frigates engaged
in the reduction of Tripoli. So well had he conducted
himself, and such trust had Captain Campbell found
him worthy of, that a few days before his nineteenth
birthday he was appointed to the command of the
Nautilus, a little schooner attached to the squadron,

and in her he had numerous adventures worth relating. To give a recounting of all of them would be to write a separate history of the war with Tripoli, and so we give but a short account of the connection of Perry's command with one of the most daring enterprises of all naval history.

There was a group of young men, all junior officers of the American fleet, scarcely more than boys, who vied with each other in deeds of daring and boldness. Probably rashness might be a good word to use in connection with some of their doings, for apparently they acted upon impulse, and counted no odds in many cases where older and wiser heads would have dictated prudence. In the little cabin of the Nautilus were gathered a group of young men, all smooth-shaven, ruddy of cheek and bright of eye. But a year or two previously they had been rollicking youngsters together in the steerage; but now most of them had epaulets on their left shoulders. The tallest of them could scarcely stand erect, so low were the deck beams overhead. Perry was sitting at the head of the table. He spoke to a slender lad with aquiline features and light hair, who sat beside him with his chin in the hollow of his hand.

" How far in do you suppose we can go before discovery, Somers? " he asked.

" It all depends," was the answer, given in a dreamy manner, as if the lad's thoughts were far away. " I'm going in until I get bows on to something that will stop me. Of course, you fellows won't go any farther than the mouth of the harbor. I hope that the night's dark, and the wind for the nor'west."

"Has the commodore decided what night we are going to try it?" put in a handsome curly-headed young fellow, placing his hand on Somers's shoulder.

"To-morrow night, I take it," was the rejoinder; "we'll probably get our orders in the morning."

One of the ship's messengers here appeared at the door of the cabin. "Boat's alongside, sir," he said, touching his cap.

"Then we'd better be going," said Decatur.

The young commander arose and escorted his guests to the deck, and they left the side with all the usual ceremonies, and shoved off into the darkness. But Perry stood there leaning against the rail for some minutes before going below. It seemed hard to imagine that it was but ten years before that he and his father had sat under the shade of the maples while he listened to the tale that had so thrilled him. He had lived not a few stories himself since that day, and now here he was in acting command of his own vessel, with responsibilities upon his shoulders, and men to jump at his very gesture of command. Somehow the expression on Somers's face haunted him— the sad, dreamy look, as if he realized for the first time fully what was before him on the morrow. He could

yet hear the roll of the oars, and a laugh broke the stillness, coming from the direction of the parting boats.
He recognized that it was Lieutenant Decatur, and
then there came another musical laugh. It was Richard
Somers this time. Perry turned and went down to
the cabin.

CHAPTER III.

PERHAPS no vessel ever bore a more fitting name or one more suited to her calling than did the bomb-ketch Intrepid. She is inseparably connected with the names of the bravest, and she marks one of the most daring enterprises of all history.*

The next day after the meeting recorded in the last chapter was the 4th of September. All day long boats were plying from the flagship to and fro to the ketch that lay at her anchor well down in the water, for her load was heavy. Before evening she had in her hold one hundred barrels of gunpowder and one hundred and fifty shells with fuses cut short to fire within a second. Lieutenant Henry Wadsworth was chosen by Somers to accompany him as second in command. Six men were to come from the Constitution's crew, and four were to be chosen from the crew of the Nautilus. With the two young officers the crew thus numbered twelve, and they

---

* The reader may be referred to another volume in the Young Heroes of Our Navy series, entitled Decatur and Somers, by Miss Molly Elliot Seawell.

were to sail that powder-laden vessel past the outside batteries under the mouths of the guns of the Crescent fort and into the Tripolitan fleet and the mass of tangled shipping that lay moored beneath the shadows of the castle. Perry stood beside Lieutenant Somers when he called for volunteers to accompany him. He never could forget the few calm words that Somers used in portraying the dangers to be faced; and when he had stopped and asked the question, "Now my lads, those who will go, step one pace forward," Perry's heart gave a great bound, and he commenced to breathe like a runner calling upon his strength. Like a regiment at drill, the ship's company, the whole sixty-two of them, stepped one pace forward, and then, as if anxious to keep in the front rank, they came silently elbowing and jostling aft to the mast where the sacred line of the quarter-deck begins. Somers knew every man on the Nautilus by name. He looked down the line, and without changing a muscle of his face spoke quietly, " James Harris." A short, thickset man, with light blue eyes and a heavy, smooth-shaven jaw, stepped forward and touched his cap. " William Keith, James Sims, Thomas Tompline." The three sailors mentioned stood beside Harris. They were fine creatures to look at, these hardy, fearless tars. The rest of the crew cast envious glances at them, and went forward to the forecastle. A fast, four-oared boat was lowered away, and the sailors and their commander made off for the ketch. Soon after dusk sail was made, and accompanied by the Nautilus, the Argus, and the Vixen, the Intrepid led the way toward the harbor mouth. As they reached it another vessel joined them. It was the Siren, under command of Lieutenant Stewart. She ventured in farther than the others, who soon lost sight of the fire-ship. Perry was standing near Lieutenant Reed, leaning against the shrouds, their eyes paining them from the strain of looking out into the darkness, when suddenly there came a glaring flash that lit the shores so that every minaret gleamed and every rope and sail could be seen on the vessels near about them. A deafening roar followed, and then all was still. The shore battery that had begun popping away at Somers's vessel—for, alas! she had been discovered very soon—stopped. Not a sound was to be heard, except the voice of an old sailor on the forecastle praying in a fervent undertone, and now all listened—listened as ears have never listened before or since.

"I hear them, I hear the oars," said a little midshipman, and all hands drew a breath.

But no, it was merely the beating of the water against the bow; no boats came speeding back to the harbor mouth. In a few minutes it was known that, whether the enemy had been discomfited or not, the brave lads in the fire-ship had met their fate. The Constitution lying in the offing began to fire minute guns. They sounded solemnly at intervals through the night. The news then came from the Constitution's steerage that little midshipman Israel was missing, and soon it was known that he had smuggled himself aboard the Intrepid in the flagship's cutter.

Who had fired the train no one knew, and no one will ever know. For days a gloom hung over the fleet. Young Lieutenant Perry could never get the idea quite from his mind that Somers felt sure that night in the cabin of the Nautilus that he should never return.

After the close of the war with Tripoli all the young officers who had so distinguished themselves found themselves back in their own country with very little to do. The United States was at peace with every nation, although strained relations were growing up between our country and Great Britain, owing to the continued impressment of American sailors.

In 1808, in retaliation for England's declaration that the coasts of Europe were in a state of blockade, an embargo was laid upon their vessels coming to our own shores, and to Lieutenant Perry was given the command of seventeen gunboats at the Newport station. For two years he continued here, and in 1810 he was given the command of the United States schooner Revenge, attached to Commodore Rogers's squadron at New London. In her he made a cruise

3

to the southward. Off the coast of Georgia he was fortunate enough to be able to come to the rescue of the crew of the ship Diana, of Wiscosset. The seamanship and judgment he displayed in handling his own vessel brought him again before the eye of the public, and he was complimented by Congress upon his action.

The Revenge was one of our crack sailing vessels of the smaller class. The young commander was more than proud of her, but ill fortune was soon to overtake him. In January, 1811, he sailed from Newport to New London, and when but a short way to the westward of Point Judith he ran into a dense fog, as he recorded in a letter to a friend at the time, "the thickest, Lord knows, I shall ever see, or, God grant, shall surround any vessel in dangerous waters." A pilot was on board who knew well the coast, and under his directions the Revenge crept slowly along through the impenetrable mists. Perry himself, becoming a little anxious, thought it better to work off shore more to the southward. The pilot declared at first that he knew well his whereabouts, and could take the vessel into the mouth of the Thames with his eyes shut and by the lead alone.

There was a heavy swell on at the time, and the lead showed deep water. Suddenly a man at the bow shouted back the startling words, "Breakers ahead!" Nothing could be seen, but the sound of

tumbling waters was heard plainly. The Revenge
was thrown up into the wind, and the anxious young
officer once more addressed the pilot. "Where are
we, sir?" he asked sternly. The poor man apparently had not only lost his bearing, but his mind.
In his fright and horror his teeth began to chatter.

"I—I do not know, sir," he faltered, and he almost collapsed upon the deck.

Immediately the anchor was dropped, but with
the set of the tide the Revenge drifted down upon
the reef, and in a few minutes she struck, stern fore-
most. The swell hove her farther in, and despite all
the efforts to kedge her off she was soon driven
broadside down, and the great waves began to break
along her bulwarks. Boats were lowered, and it
was ascertained that she lay off the mouth of the
Pawcatuck River. To the northward lay what is
known as Watch Hill.

The good judgment of Perry was now shown.
Nothing, he perceived, could keep his vessel from
destruction, and he determined to save as much
property as he possibly could. Soon all boats were
out. The personal belongings of officers and crew
were taken ashore; the sails and spars were put
over the side; even the guns were placed on rafts,
and the smaller ones taken ashore in boats, and before the vessel began to show signs of breaking up
he had stripped her and dismantled her of almost

everything; nothing but a sheer hulk lay there, to be devoured by the hungry sea.

Perry demanded a court of inquiry into his conduct upon this occasion, despite the fact that he was relieved of blame by all his officers and men. The court, after a full investigation, decided that his conduct was not only free from blame but deserving of great praise. So, although he lost his ship, he lost nothing of his reputation.

Again he returned to Newport, and here he married a Miss Mason, the beautiful daughter of Dr. Mason of that city. But during this time war with England was becoming more and more of a certainty, and when it was declared, to young Perry was again given the command of a flotilla of gunboats stationed for the protection of Rhode Island waters. It was not a very active position, and the situation of being practically unemployed was extremely galling to a man of his ambition and keen desires. So, hearing of the organization of the naval forces under the command of Commodore Chauncey upon the lakes, he solicited permission to join them, and was ordered to repair to Sackett's Harbor, on Lake Ontario, where part of the fleet was being fitted out.

CHAPTER IV.

IT was a fortunate thing that the United States Government perceived very early the importance of securing the command of the Great Lakes. Although the country that they bordered upon was wild in the extreme, and both shores were thronged with hostile and semi-hostile Indians, nevertheless the few settlements that had grown up in the wilderness were of great importance to the United States, and the lakes were the key to the possession of the power upon our Northwestern frontier.

In the month of October, 1812, Commodore Chauncey, whom the Government had chosen as the man best fitted for the purpose, had proceeded to Lake Ontario. The long, wearisome march through the wilderness of the force that accompanied him would make a history in itself; but at last he arrived upon the shores of the great waters, and found himself in command of about seven hundred seamen and one hundred and fifty marines. When they arrived, a strange state of affairs existed. Shipbuilders and carpenters had been at work for some months. From

green timber and newly felled trees they had constructed a number of vessels, and out of the primitive
forest had made shipyards, and the noise of hammer
and saw resounded from daylight to dark. But the
prospects for success were extremely gloomy. One of
the first vessels launched, a brig named Adams, after
the illustrious patriot of Massachusetts, had fallen into
the hands of the British soon after the unfortunate
surrender of the American General Hull, who, for
some reason best known to himself and never fully
explained, had turned over the forces at his command
to the British almost without striking a blow. Owing
to the early descent of winter, but little could be done
in the way of placing the American fleet upon a war
footing, and the spring of the year 1813 found
the British in almost undisputed control of the water
ways. But several incidents had occurred during this
time which it is not possible to pass by in this connection without a mention, and one of these is the capture of the British brigs Detroit and Caledonia, the
former being the name that the enemy had given to
the Adams after she had fallen into their hands; and
although this has little to do with the story of Perry
himself, it tells an interesting chapter of what happened, and shows the caliber of the men that he was
subsequently called to command. The British had
built and manned several forts composed of logs and
wood, on the northern shore, and as bases of supplies

they served good purpose in the forays and expeditions against the Americans to the southward. On
the 7th of October the Detroit and the Caledonia
sailed down the lake and anchored under the guns of
Fort Erie. Lieutenant Elliot (of whom more hereafter) was at Buffalo, superintending the purchase and
outfitting of some vessels that it was intended should
be attached to the American flotilla. The news was
brought to him that the British vessels had been
sighted and were lying at anchor within view of the
American shore. Immediately he rode out to the encampment of General Smyth and informed him of the
circumstance, and asked permission to organize a cut-
ting-out party and capture both ships by surprise
under the cover of darkness. General Smyth listened
attentively to the plan, and then shook his head doubt-
fully.

"I doubt, sir," said he, "whether there are above
a score of men in my command who can pull an oar,
or who would be of the slightest use to you in a boat
attack. I can not order my carpenters and shipbuilders
to your support, for their services are too valuable to
be risked in such a venture."

"It is indeed a shame for such a chance to be
passed by without attempting something," responded
Lieutenant Elliot, "for information has been brought
to me that, although the Detroit is manned by but
fifty-six Englishmen, she has on board thirty American

prisoners; and the Caledonia, with a crew of but twelve, has ten good Americans on board of her. The liberation of these men, even if accomplished by a boarding party of landsmen, would insure a force sufficient for the working of both vessels."

But again General Smyth shook his head. A landsman on the water, in his idea, was at much greater disadvantage than a seaman ashore. While this conversation was in progress a figure was seen approaching upon a jaded horse, and immediately news was brought that a detachment of sailors, who had marched over five hundred miles from the Hudson River, was in camp some thirty-two miles away to the eastward. It was near nightfall, but nevertheless Elliot persuaded the General to dispatch a rider at once with orders for the seamen to hasten and take up again their weary tramp.   Long before daylight the foot-sore Jackies were again on the move, and by noon they came straggling into the camp.   A sorry-looking lot they were indeed.   No one would ever have taken them for a ship's company of jaunty tars; their clothes were in rags, and by the hard and unaccustomed work of the past few weeks they had been worn almost to skin and bone.   They bore no arms, and some of them were so weak that they could scarce keep on their feet, and leaned upon one another for support.   The well-fed soldiers looked at them with pity. They appeared to be more like candidates for the hospital than men from whom a fight might be expected. It seemed impossible to call upon these men for further exertion; it seemed cruel to ask them to perform even the lightest duty. But Elliot knew the stuff that they were made of. Under the direction of the carpenters, two small boats carrying about fifty men apiece had been prepared for active service. Smyth, who had inspected the forlorn detachment with Elliot, again looked extremely dubious.

"When do you suppose that these poor fellows will be ready or able to perform any work?" he asked, after he had carefully looked over the band of unarmed and dusty wayfarers, mere tramps and vagrants, to all appearances.

"This very day," Elliot responded, "and by tomorrow morning I will have those ships, or know the reason why."

When a sailor is expected to perform any especially arduous duty, the first thing that his officers do is to see that he is well fed, and an extra feeding means that extra work is intended for him. Hence the royal spread that was provided for the almost exhausted sailors might have warned them that their services were soon to be made use of. Three hours after their arrival in camp the poor fellows were told that they would have to forego sleep and rest, for orders were given immediately for a picked body of them to man the two boats, and, without being fully informed of

the service ahead of them, they were crowded on
board. It was then found that in the whole detachment there were no boarding pikes, cutlasses, or battle-
axes, weapons with which they were familiar and knew
well how to use. Only twenty pistols could be pro-
cured; muskets in their hands were of little use, as
they were but little acquainted with this style of
weapon. The boats proceeded a short distance down
Buffalo Creek, and then were made fast to the bank.
General Smyth had attached two small companies of
infantry, numbering twenty-five, to each boat to aid the
sailors in their expedition. It seemed almost heart-
less to call upon the latter to make any movement.
Lying huddled together in their dusty rags they slept
like dead men. But shortly after midnight they were
aroused, and those most capable of exertion were
placed upon the thwarts, the oars were manned, and
with the sluggish current they pulled out into the
waters of the lake. For two hours steadily they rowed,
and when a poor fellow would fall over at his work
another was ordered and urged into his place. At
three o'clock the word was passed back from the bow
that the two vessels were in sight. This seemed to
stir all hands to action. Grumbling stopped, and with
muffled oars and in dead silence the boats came gliding
alongside—the leader making for the Caledonia, which
was anchored nearer inshore, and the second boarding
party aiming for the main chains of the Detroit.

The midnight surprise of the Detroit.

Elliot had not reckoned wrongly. No doubt it had been a comfort to the men themselves to find that a naval officer was in charge of them. It inspired them with a confidence that otherwise they might not have had. The familiar orders awakened them from their lethargy. When the boats grated alongside of the unsuspecting ships every man was alert, and with a will they tumbled on board. Only one or two shots were fired. It was a complete surprise. Everything had been arranged. One party had been ordered to cut the cable, another to confine the Englishmen, and another to liberate the American prisoners in the hold; a fourth was to make sail upon the vessels, in order to carry them, if possible, up the river and out of the reach of the guns of Fort Erie. But alas! often the best-laid plans go astray, and the very thing needed to make the expedition a success failed them completely. There was no wind. The sails hung listlessly against the masts, and as soon as the cables were cut by the swift blows of the axes both vessels gathered stern way and drifted with the current down the stream closer to the shore and almost into the mouths of the English guns. The fort immediately opened fire upon them with grape and solid shot at the closest range, but owing to the darkness and the suddenness of the surprise, perhaps, the gunners found little time to train their pieces effectively, for, strange as it may seem, the first volley did but little damage. Below the fort in the woods were scattered at intervals several pieces of flying artillery, and as the vessels came in sight, ambushed by the trees and hidden from view, they began a most effective fire. The Caledonia had managed to get out sweeps and had crept out into the river. Soon she was beached on a little point of land known as Black Rock, in as near a position as possible to one of the American batteries on the southern shore. But the Detroit, that Elliot now commanded, being the heavier vessel, could not be handled so easily. She drifted down the river, a target for every gun on shore, and at daybreak she found herself in a most unhappy position. By this time, even if the wind had sprung up, the sails would have afforded but slight assistance. They were riddled with shot, and most of the yards and stays were carried away. In sheer despair Elliot dropped a spare anchor from the bows and hove to short, within four hundred yards of an English battery, whose guns could be seen plainly extending above the ramparts of logs and earth. An officer in a red coat stepped out in plain view.

"Surrender where you are," he shouted, "or I'll blow you out of water!"

It looked as if there was nothing else to do but to comply. The overworked sailors listened for their commander's words. It would indeed seem hard if, after their toilsome march and the sudden and exacting duty, they should find themselves prisoners so soon.

Perhaps Elliot's reply can not be taken seriously, at all events his subsequent actions belied the words he spoke.

"If you dare fire a shot into me," he cried, mounting the rail, "I'll bring all the prisoners on deck, and their blood be on your heads!"

In reply, the guns spoke. But the prisoners were left where it was no doubt Elliot's intention they should be, down in the hold.

Again the cable was cut, and the guns on his starboard hand were brought to bear with some effect upon the English battery.

But bad news was brought to him. The ammunition was exhausted! He had not enough left to fire a single round, and in addition it was learned that the pilot, a French Canadian, and the only person on board who understood anything of the currents and shoals of the river, had disappeared, probably slipping into the water and swimming ashore. Helpless and well-nigh hopeless, the Detroit drifted down the stream; but fortunately, before she had passed the battery, she struck a cross current and headed for the southern shore. In fifteen minutes she grounded on Squaw Island, little more than halfway to safety. The stream ran swiftly in broken rapids between the island and the American side. The shots from the English guns could reach the stranded vessel, but despite the danger and while he was still under fire, Elliot lowered his boats, and placing the prisoners in them first, he succeeded in ferrying all his men to the shelter of the friendly land, the last boat reaching there at about eight o'clock in the morning. Before noon a company of British regulars rowed out from the Canadian shore, and in turn boarded the deserted vessel, but a party of volunteers, composed of a detachment of Yankee troops under Major Chapin, drove them back before the flames were started, for it was the intention of the English to set the Detroit on fire. In the afternoon they made another attempt, but were again repulsed. Then it was determined, owing to the fact that she was badly grounded, that the Americans in their turn should set her on fire. When they had relieved her of her stores and equipment as much as possible, she was given over to the flames. The little Caledonia was saved, and she proved to be no inconsiderable prize, for, in addition to her guns and well-stored magazine, she had on board a cargo of furs whose value has been estimated at one hundred and fifty thousand dollars.

What would Elliot have done in this affair had it not been for the arrival of the men from the seacoast, the Yankee sailors, the brave fellows to whom the country owed almost everything before the war was ended?—these bold-hearted, tireless lads, who had accomplished more than one could almost expect of human beings, who had fought without resting and gone without sleep and food, willingly taking up their duties, suffering hardships almost unequaled. These were the men that Perry found himself at the head of when he came to take command of the flotilla upon the lakes. How they behaved under him, and what they accomplished, make the best part of this story.

CHAPTER V.

THE YOUNG COMMANDER.

IT was in March, 1813, that Oliver Hazard Perry received his appointment as master commandant, and shortly afterward his application for active service on the lakes was granted, and he set out with all speed for Sackett's Harbor, at the port of Erie, where the American fleet was in progress of completion. He arrived there late in the month of March. Winter was still on; deep drifts were in the roads and woods; the ice still thick in the lakes. For a month the young officer found plenty to do in superintending the placing of the armaments on board of the vessels and rushing the work in order to be ready to get afloat and in active service in early spring. On the 23d of April he learned of the intention of Commodore Chauncey and General Dearborn, in command of the troops, to attack Fort George, an English stronghold not far from Queenstown. On the 25th of April he proceeded from Sackett's Harbor and joined the commodore at Niagara, and no doubt his advice, his bravery, and skill were of the greatest benefit in effecting the reduction of the fort. The plans were exceedingly well arranged. On the night of the 26th, under cover of darkness, the fort had been reconnoitered and small buoys placed at varying distances in order to designate the positions that the American vessels should take in the action.

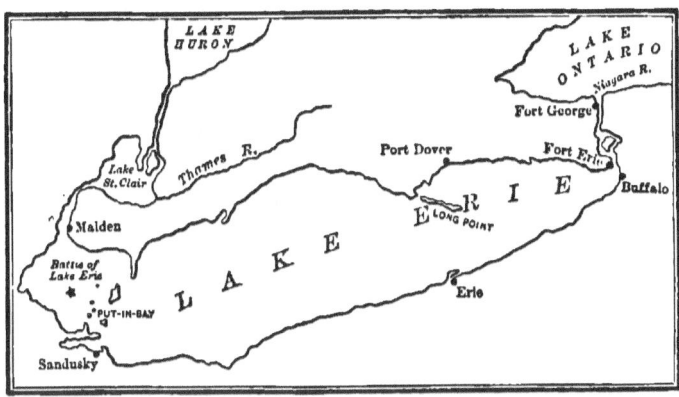

Lake Erie.

At three o'clock in the morning of the 27th the fleet started. The larger vessels, named the Madison, Oneida, and Lady of the Lake, took on board most of the heavy artillery and as many troops as they could carry. The rest of the attacking force crowded into the smaller boats, and by daylight the schooners had found their moorings and opened fire upon the enemy's batteries. So well served and aimed were the guns that in ten minutes the return fire of the English was seen to be slacking, and before a quarter of an hour of cannonading they retreated back into the

woods, abandoning their position. In the meantime
the American infantry had been landed near one of the
forts that had been reduced at a point called Two-mile
Creek. The landing occurred without opposition, but
the troops had not advanced far before they received
a tremendous fire from the woods, and the British appeared in force along the edge of the steep bank up
which the Americans were making their way. The
schooners poured a withering fire into them over
the heads of their own men and once more caused
them to scatter. They retreated immediately to
Fort George, where they blew up their magazines,
and, setting fire to what stores they could not carry
away, they made off in great haste to Queenstown.
For some distance they were chased by the light
infantry, but at last pursuit was abandoned, and
the American forces joined together again at Fort
George.

Perry was practically a volunteer in this action;
but the commodore referred to his services in the most
highly flattering terms. He shunned no danger, and
it was remarked that he must have worn a charm
against bullets, for many times, regardless of his safety, he had practically offered himself as a target, but
the missiles scattered around him, leaving him unscathed.

All this preliminary description is absolutely necessary to the leading up to the happenings of the early

"Ready! All ready, your honor!" (Commodore Perry at the battle of Lake Erie)

From an engraving by W. Ridgway after J. R. Chapin

fall, the glorious occasion when Perry won for himself
the title that greeted him wherever he went during
his lifetime, that of the " Hero of Erie."

The day after the fall of Fort George, Perry was
dispatched by the commodore with a body of fifty-
five seamen to Black Rock, where he was ordered to
take charge of the five vessels at that place and
proceed with them at once to the port of Erie.
He was urged to have the whole squadron prepared
and ready for orders and action at the earliest possible moment. With two hundred soldiers that
General Dearborn placed on board the vessels at
Black Rock, Perry sailed early in June, intending
to join his little fleet with those already under his
command at Erie.

The British had two splendidly equipped and fast-
sailing vessels waiting to intercept the little squadron.
They were named the Lady Provost and the Queen
Charlotte. At a place called Long Point, where the
channel is exceedingly narrow, they lay anchored in
midstream keeping a vigilant lookout; but their wake-
fulness availed them nothing, for on a dark night Perry
succeeded in passing them, drifting by within one hundred yards of the Queen Charlotte. Their chagrin at
the escape of the flotilla they had considered already
in their power can readily be imagined.

In May Perry's largest vessels, which he named the
Niagara and the Lawrence, were launched, and every

exertion was made to complete their equipment and fit them for service. On July 22d the commodore arrived at the head of Lake Ontario and sent one hundred and seventy seamen down to Perry, who was glad enough to gain their services. Just at this time the English vessels were off the mouth of the port of Erie, within plain sight of the town. One or two of the American gunboats sailed out to reconnoiter them, and a few shots were exchanged at long range, without any damage being done to one side or the other. The vessels now under the command of the young commodore, although he only held his title by courtesy, consisted of the Lawrence, Niagara, Caledonia, Ariel, Scorpion, and Somers. Two smaller vessels, named the Congress and Porcupine, were nearly completed, and were put in commission early in the month of August. The British squadron, hovering outside of the port, received information that caused them much delight; for they were well informed in regard to the progress in the construction of the American vessels, and knew well the difficulties which lay before them.

It was known that the water on the long sandy bar crossing the mouth of the river was exceedingly shallow, but a few inches over six feet, in the ordinary condition of the stream. The Niagara drew nine feet, and the Lawrence nine feet four inches, which rendered them absolutely useless, the English thought, and

placed them in the position of stranded ships or prisoners unless they could escape from their position. To
dig a channel sufficiently wide and deep would be almost a hopeless task, and so the English commodore
chuckled to himself. But Perry went on with his
preparations undisturbed, and as if entirely in igno-
rance of the fact that he had become a laughing-stock
for the British. At the appointed time the smaller vessels proceeded down stream and crossed the bar, and
as soon as everything was in order the Niagara and
the Lawrence followed them and anchored bow and
stern but a few rods above where the shallows began.
Four large scows were now towed downstream and
placed one on either side of the imprisoned ships. The
plugs were drawn from their bottoms, the water entered, and each scow sank until only a few inches of
the bulwarks were above the surface. In this position they were secured by heavy beams thrust through
the ports of the two vessels, the plugs were replaced,
and then by means of pumps and active bailing the
water in the scows was put over the side, and buoyantly
they rose, lifting with tremendous power the vessels
between them, and reducing their draft to such a measure that in safety they crossed the bar, amid the shouts
of the people on shore and the cheers of the sailors of
the fleet.

The feelings of the officers of his Majesty who had
indulged in the hilarity before mentioned are not de-

scribed in history, but soon they must have learned
of the occurrence.

Now Perry had the ships, but he lacked the men
to handle them, and how could he secure sailors up
there in the wilderness?   There was but one way open
for him, and that was to make them out of the rough
material from which the troops (mostly militia) were
drawn.   He received permission to call for volunteers
from among the Pennsylvania lads, and from the body
who offered themselves he picked some seventy or
eighty.   The British blockading squadron had with-
drawn, and Perry put out with this nondescript force
and what actually amounted to a practice cruise.   The
men were exercised at the guns and taught such seamanship as was considered necessary, and upon their
return to Erie they were a little more handy and somewhat acquainted with their duties, but yet they were a
good deal like the wood of which the vessels was principally composed, a trifle green.

On the last day in August orders were received to
join with the land forces of General Harrison and assist
in the reduction of the town of Malden on the Canadian
shore.   In accordance with this plan Perry sailed, and
held an interview with General Harrison, in which he
succeeded in persuading the latter to detail some of
his most expert riflemen on board the fleet to act in
the capacity of marines, a force in which he was entirely deficient.   The general, recognizing the useful-

ness of such a corps, detailed seventy Kentuckians to
go on board the ships, and these men subsequently
rendered good accounts of themselves, as will be told.

Owing to the fact that the Ohio had been dispatched
to Erie after provisions, and that the Amelia (a
little sailing craft) had been left behind because of the
lack of men to man her, Perry's force now consisted
of nine sail mounting in all fifty-four guns. In the
harbor of Malden lay the British fleet, smaller in the
number of vessels but heavier in armament, consisting
of six vessels carrying sixty-six guns. It was intended
that Perry should tempt them to leave the protection
of the forts and meet him in the open waters of the
lake, and that General Harrison should then attack
the town by land. But the British commodore refused the offer to engage, although the Yankee squadron sailed up and down in plain sight, flying all their
bunting.

At last, seeing that it was fruitless, the plan was
abandoned, and Perry sailed back into Put-in-Bay, distance some thirty-four miles. Here he dropped anchor.
It had been thought unwise to risk a battle on land
until the supremacy of the water ways should be settled
by a decisive engagement. Without doubt this same
thought was in the minds of the British, and on their
part every preparation was hastened to place their vessels in condition for the coming struggle. In speaking
of the period of suspense that preceded the great fight

of the 10th of September, a contemporary refers to the
attitude of the commanders of the two squadrons as
follows:

"What must have been their reflections during this
interval we will not undertake to conjecture. There are
few spectacles more sublime, and none more impressive, than that of two hostile armies, or two hostile
fleets, situated in the neighborhood of each other, re-
posing only as preparatory to commencing the awful
work of death. It is an awful pause, and a calm which
appears most profound from the minds associating it
with what is to follow, just as the stillness is the greatest
which precedes the tempest. This scene is more sublime and impressive than that of the same hostile parties
when engaged in battle. Then other sensations are
produced—those of horror and sympathy, of hope and
fear—all the passions being greatly agitated. But during the repose which precedes an engagement the
mind is cool, unagitated, and susceptible of deep impressions from the impending storm, upon which the
fate of thousands of our fellow-men, and sometimes the
destiny of nations, may depend. If such would be the
impressions of an observer, what must be the feelings
of those who are about to engage themselves in the
'bloody strife'?"

All this is very fine old-fashioned writing; but it
was indeed a momentous occasion, for, although separate actions had been fought at sea, upon no occasion

had fleets of both countries been engaged. The English officers were men of experience in such affairs, men who had served with Nelson, well versed in line maneuvering and strategy. On the other hand, the Americans were commanded by young officers, few of whom had seen actual service, and the sailors and landsmen were all untried. Perry felt that the honor and reputation of his country were in his keeping. He knew that the conflict could not be long deferred, but he did not anticipate that the English would be the first to move in the game.

Shortly after sunrise on the 10th of September a messenger knocked at his cabin door. The English fleet was in sight!

CHAPTER VI.

THE FLAGSHIP.

MASTER-COMMANDANT PERRY was up in an instant. He hurried into his uniform and ascended to the deck. It was yet gray in the morning; a faint line of rosy light stretched above the hilltops to the eastward, promising the dawning of a glorious day. A thin mist hung over the water, scarcely moved by the light breeze that was blowing from the northward. Everything looked so calm and peaceful and so commonplace that the young commodore could scarcely bring himself to believe that this was to be the most important crisis of his life. There is an unreality attached to early dawn, with its broadening, lifting twilight, and the change which comes swiftly, until suddenly, as it were, like a burst of music after a few distant and preliminary chords, the great day opens. On shore the news had not spread among the houses, and they stood there gray and silent. From a few chimneys rose little columns of smoke, showing that the early housewife had begun her daily duties. But nearer to hand, among the vessels of the fleet all was bustle and preparation. There were hoarse shouts and orders, the cheeping of block and tackle, hails and counter-hails, and the thrum of oars, as the small boats plied busily back and forth from one vessel to another.

Perry had sent orders for Lieutenant Elliot to repair on board the Lawrence as soon as possible; at once Elliot came alongside. He was evidently laboring under much excitement.

"The day has come at last!" he said.

"The one we have long been wishing for," Perry returned.

There was very little time to lay out a plan of campaign, but nevertheless it was arranged that the vessels should keep as well in line as possible, and that the flagship should be in the van. She was the largest of the Yankee fleet, and most suited for the honor. Perry saw Elliot over the side, and then he turned to Lieutenant Brooks, a tall and exceedingly handsome young officer, and after ordering him to make sail and signal the rest of the fleet to follow, he asked if the flag that he had ordered had been finished.

"I have it here," Brooks returned, "and the quartermaster is bending it to the halyards."

Perry gave a smile of satisfaction as an instant later a great blue flag rose swiftly to the masthead. On it in large white letters that could be read at almost the distance of a mile were the last words of the brave James Lawrence, "DON'T GIVE UP THE SHIP!"

It rippled out bravely in the light morning air, and
as the Lawrence gained headway and sailed past the
others to take her position as the leader every boat
broke out into cheers. Now from the shore these
cheers were answered, for the people had begun to
gather on the hillsides, and from several tall trees flew
little American flags. Yet there was nothing warlike
in the scene. It might have been, to all appearances,
gazing at it from a distance, a gala festival. But on
board the ships things wore a different look. The
men had a fierce impetuosity about them as they
worked or spoke. Some were palpably nervous, and
the piles of shot and the charges of powder that were
being brought up from the magazines showed what
business was expected. Beyond the mouth of the bay
appeared the English fleet, a beautiful sight indeed.
The sun caught their sails and changed their colors
from dull gray to pink. Their flags were flying, and
they were approaching in one long line, the largest
leading. Their numbers and their strength were
known to the American officers.

The first vessel was the Detroit, carrying nineteen
guns; next came the Queen Charlotte, carrying seventeen guns; then the Lady Provost, named in compli-
ment to the wife of Sir Charles Provost, the English
leader; then followed the brig Hunter, of ten guns; the
sloop Little Belt, of three; and the small schooner
Chippewa, that boasted of but one. The breeze was so

light, and the fleets were so far apart, that it would
be some hours before the engagement could possibly
begin. Perry turned as he suddenly heard a question
addressed to him. He looked down at the figure that
stood at his elbow, literally and not figuratively, as it
reached scarcely higher—a bright little boy of but thir-
teen or fourteen, in white canvas trousers, and a wide
black tie loosely flowing in the wind over his shoulder.
He wore a short roundabout jacket with brass buttons,
and his long curly hair stood out on each side of his big
midshipman's cap. It was Perry's little brother, a boy
of great spirit. He resembled the young commodore
in coloring and feature. It seemed hardly possible that
any one so young and innocent could be brought
into such doings, or asked to face the dangers of
deadly action. He pointed his hand out over the
bulwarks.

"See those wild ducks," he said; "they look as
if they were telling us to come on—don't they?"

Some brilliantly colored wild fowl, alarmed by the
approach of the fleet, clattered up out of the water
and swept past the flagship's bows, heading directly
for the English sail. It is a strange thing that in moments of great suspense or excitement small incidents
like this impress themselves upon the mind. The boy
had no thought of approaching danger; he had no
idea what death and destruction he might soon be wit-
nessing. His trust and dependence and his admira-

tion for his elder brother made him feel perfectly safe. Somehow it reminded the young commodore of the way he felt when on the General Greene with his own father in command.

"Youngster," he said, "we may soon be fighting; stay close by me."

"I'll be right here," returned the little fellow, "where you can find me."

The Lawrence had now gained the position that Perry wished her to hold, and he turned to look back at the line of his little fleet. He had more vessels in his squadron than the English in theirs, as we have said, but the guns he carried were less in number, amounting to a total of fifty-four, while, as it was afterward proved, the enemy mounted sixty-three. Not far from the Lawrence sailed the brig Niagara, that Elliot commanded. Like the flagship, she carried twenty guns, all carronades, useless at long range, but terribly destructive when within pistol shot. Just beyond the Niagara was the Caledonia, the vessel that had been captured; she mounted three guns. The schooner Ariel mounted four, and then followed the gunboats in a body. The Scorpion and the Somers carried two guns each on their unprotected decks, for the bulwarks were scarcely the height of a man's knee; the Tigress and the Porcupine, schooners also, each carried one carronade. A jaunty little single-sticker, the Tripp, of one

gun, sailed along with them. It was but a toy
fleet, to all appearances.

The Englishmen had the weather gauge, and were
coming bravely on as fast as the light air would per-
mit them. But at ten o'clock the breeze died away,
and although both sides were eager to begin the fighting, they drifted at safe distance, watching one another and longing to be at it. Then in a few minutes the wind, which had veered to the southwest,
again changed direction, as it often does on the inland
waters, and blew offshore from the southeast, giving
the American squadron the advantage that had been
held heretofore by the enemy, that of the weather
gauge. Slowly they forged along toward the waiting
English fleet. The order was now slightly changed.
The two little gunboats Scorpion and Ariel were now
in the lead but a pistol-shot distance off the port bow
of the Lawrence, whose motto flag was fluttering and
tossing in the bright sunlight. Soon they were leading
the rest by over a quarter of a mile, and it was evident that one would be the first to engage the enemy.
The suspense increased. The men were all at their
quarters; some of the old sailors had stripped themselves to the waist, as they did in the old-time
style. Here was a gun crew standing quietly about
their piece; and lining the bulwarks were a crowd
of motley uniforms—riflemen from Kentucky in fringed
shirts and buckskin leggings stood next to regular

soldiers in their brass and leather shakos, militia-
men in homemade uniforms, nervously fingering their
clumsy flintlock muskets, but all bravely determined
to stand by their young commander to the last. Down

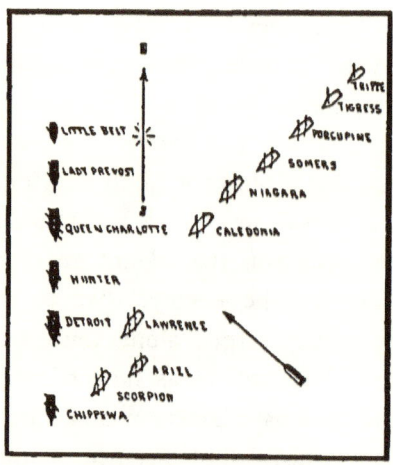

Diagram of the battle, No. 1.

in the little cockpit the surgeon, Usher Parsons, had
spread his tables and made ready his shining knives
and instruments. There was scarcely head room in
his deadly workshop, and alas! owing to the light
draught of the vessel, it was not, as it should have
been, safe below the water line.

Lieutenants Yarnell and Brooks were on the quarter-deck, talking in loud voices and counting the moments when the first gun should be fired. They had
not long to wait. At fifteen minutes before twelve

the nearest Englishman, the Detroit, opened fire, dis-
charging a single gun. The aim was good; the ball
struck with a shock in the Lawrence's bow. It did
no damage, but a most unfortunate circumstance occurred. The slight breeze died away at this instant, and it fell dead calm. It had been Perry's
intention boldly to break the British line and to
have the rest of his vessels follow him into close
action; and it must be stated in all justice that close
action was what the British commodore, brave Captain Barclay one of the men who had fought with
Nelson at the Nile, desired most also. He was not
the man to shirk this style of fighting. For a minute
there was a pause. Perry looked back at the rest of
his vessels and almost groaned. There they lay,
swinging hither and thither, with their sails hanging
lifeless, too far off to be of the slightest assistance to
him. Again the Detroit fired, and now those who
had never been in action before caught their first sight
of blood. The ball struck the edge of one of the
after ports, partly dismounted the gun, killed the man
standing at the lock, and filled the air with a shower
of splinters. A man staggered aft with both hands
clasped about his neck, where he had been pierced as
though by an arrow. One of the flying bits of wood
caught Lieutenant Yarnell on the brow; he staggered
slightly, and dashed away the blood. Taking a ban-
danna handkerchief out of his pocket, he tossed his big

5

hat to one side and tightly bound up the wound without a word. Yarnell was dressed like a common sailor;
in fact, few of the officers wore any distinguishing
uniform, and Perry was bareheaded during most of
the engagement. In reply to this death-dealing shot,
one of the guns of the forward division was fired,
and then it was seen how horrible the position of
the flagship was at the moment. The carronade
that had replied was impotent; the ball carried
scarcely more than two thirds of the way to its
mark, and plashed harmlessly into the water. Another was fired, with the same result. Perry turned
to Brooks.

"Cease firing," he said; "it is wasting powder and
shot. O God, give us some wind, that we may come
up with them!"

But no wind came, and the Detroit with her
long guns kept up her practice gunnery. The other
vessels joined in. But for ten minutes not a lock-
string was pulled on board the Lawrence. Blocks
and rigging fell from aloft, splinters were everywhere,
pools of blood covered the decks, wounded men
were being carried down the hatchways. What a
frightful thing it must have been to witness on this
beautiful, bright day, with the sky free from a single
cloud, and the sunshine lighting the hills and tree tops
along the shore! The dead soon began to encum-
ber the decks, and it became a horrible necessity

The battle on Lake Erie.

(From an engraving inscribed to Commodore Perry, his officers, and gallant crews, in 1815.)

to put them over the side, and soon the water in
close proximity was dotted with floating, mangled
bodies.

But there was no thought of surrender in the
mind of a single man on board. All Perry wished
and prayed for was to gain a position where he
could fight back in return, and with delight he saw
that he was drifting nearer and nearer. In a few
minutes it would be " give " as well as " take." The men
still stuck to their posts. Signal flags were flying from
the Lawrence's yardarm ordering the fleet in the rear
to come up and support her, but the wind was yet
too light; they could not approach. At five minutes of twelve the Lawrence began to open fire,
and the men who had hitherto remained silent started
cheering. The rattle of musketry sounded along
her bulwarks. They were breathing *their own smoke
now*, and no longer that of the enemy alone. Helpless, and unable to work a single sail—for every
brace and bowline was shot away—the Yankee flagship drifted straight in among the British vessels.
Her shots began to tell; the topmast of one of the
English brigs came down to the deck. Yarnell was
again wounded, and his features now were almost
unrecognizable. Perry ordered him below to the
surgeon, but in two minutes he returned. From
the shore and from the other vessels, which were
doing their best to come into action, the scene was

grand, if terrible. There the flagship floated; her motto flag still flying, single-handed engaging the English fleet. From every side came flashes and the thundering discharges. She was assailed from all directions, but she would not down.

CHAPTER VII.

THE BATTLE.

THERE were now seven guns that Perry found he could use in replying to the concentrated fire of the English, who had thirty-two playing upon his almost defenseless vessel. Seeing that they could now fight back, the crew had settled themselves, and were taking the death and destruction dealt everywhere about them as if it were a matter of course. A militiaman who had never been on board a craft larger than a flatboat before in all his life, and had never till three or four days previously seen a square-rigged ship, mounted into the rigging; holding his rifle under his arm, he ascended to the crosstrees, and squatting there began to load and fire with as much carelessness of his surroundings as if the feat had been practiced by him time and time before.

Seeing that it was impossible to hasten the arrival of the other vessels, who were doing their best to get into action, and knowing that the surrender of the Lawrence would be a death-blow to all chances of ultimate victory, Perry determined to hold out to the last. He did not have to tell this to the noble crew who served under him; they felt it and knew it as well as he. Never was there a sign of the white feather shown. The vessel was quivering beneath the blows she was sustaining. Some of the English shots went clean through her, carrying the deadly splinters in their wake.

Turning to give an order to Lieutenant Yarnell, the commodore almost gasped in horror, for the lieutenant's features were again almost indistinguishable. He had received another wound in the face, and was bleeding so that he was almost blinded.

"Go below, sir, to the surgeon," Perry ordered the second time.

Yarnell hesitated. "Time is precious, sir," he mumbled. But upon Perry's repeating the command he hurried down the ladder.

Lieutenant Brooks, who was in charge of the after division, came up. A grim smile was on his handsome face. "So far, so good, sir," he said. "See how our men fight! I believe we'll hold them till the rest come up."

"God grant so!" Perry replied fervently.

At this minute three men, who were serving one of the most effective guns, came down together in a heap. Their piece had just been sighted. Brooks stepped forward hastily and pulled the lanyard. It failed to go off. The captain of the gun, an old sailor, with grizzled hair and rugged features, smeared and blackened with gunpowder, began fumbling at the lock. Perry stepped close to him.

"What's the matter here, my man?" he asked, in the same cool tone that he might have used at drill.

"My piece behaves shamefully, shamefully!" the old sailor replied with the petulance of a child.

"Stand to one side, my lad," put in Lieutenant Brooks.

As he stepped up he drew a pistol from his belt, and placing the muzzle close to the priming pulled the trigger. The roar and explosion followed.

"That found the mark, sir!" cried the old sailor. "Now, my hearties, run her in!"

Lieutenant Brooks and little Midshipman Perry laid hold of the tackle, as the old sailor picked up the sponge, for the gun was now short-handed. But their places were soon filled by the gun's crew from one of the forward divisions whose piece had been dismounted. As they stepped over the bodies of their dead comrades they all looked in the face of the young captain—in fact, everywhere he found all eyes directed at him; not mutely appealing to him to save them or stop the appalling death, but as if they said, "Say but the word, sir; we're here to do our duty, and we'll die for it." It was the old *morituri te salutant,* only it was for a nobler, grander purpose than to amuse the rabble of the arena side.

Their country was the stake, their countrymen's eyes were on them. They could not and would not flinch; even the wounded who could stand tried to struggle back to their posts. It was grand, it was sublime; it was a war in all its horrible cruelty.

Again Brooks spoke to Perry.

"Noble fellows, noble fellows," he murmured, the tears standing in his eyes. "See," he suddenly exclaimed, "here comes my little negro Sam!"

A colored boy of about fourteen years of age ran up from below with a charge of powder in his hands. Brooks spoke to him encouragingly, and the little fellow grinned from ear to ear.

"You're a good boy, Sam. Don't let that gun be waiting."

"No, massa, we keeps her barkin' all de time."

Suddenly Perry felt a touch upon his hand. He looked down. It was his little brother who had grasped him, not in fear, but half unconsciously, as a child in times of excitement shows confidence and trust in a person whom it loves. A strange picture the two must have presented, both brothers so young, and yet, with such a difference in their ages, standing there hand in hand. All at once the midshipman let go his grasp and gave a cry of horror. Something heavy struck against Perry's side and was flung across the deck; he turned quickly and saw a horrible sight. There lay poor Brooks, who had been hurled against the rail. A round shot had struck him in the hip; what had been a fine, stalwart man was now a shattered wreck. His face was contracted, and in spite of all his efforts he could not control a cry of anguish and despair. The agony he suffered was terrible. Perry hastened to him.

"I'm done for, sir," he cried, "I'm done for. Have me shot, have me put out of this misery; for the sake of mercy, kill me!"

"Hush—be brave," Perry cried, grasping the lieutenant's hand. "Be brave, old friend."

As if all this was not enough to unnerve even the stoutest heart, at this very moment the little mulatto boy came running by. He stopped, and saw who it was upon the deck. The shriek he gave made some of the men at the guns turn around and look.

"Massa, O my massa, dey's done gone killed you!" he cried, bursting into a paroxysm of grief.

Brooks's face was now set and calm. "Be quiet, Sam," he said. "Go, do your duty."

Two sailors under Perry's orders picked up the mangled body from the deck and carried it below; but the little negro boy did not cease his lamentations. Maybe it was the force of habit that made him do what he did, but still crying out, "Massa, massa, oh, dey's killed my massa!" he picked up the lieutenant's heavy hat from the deck and followed the sailors and their burden down the ladder.

In recounting war and the deeds that are done
in battle, and the sights and sounds, it is necessary
to bring out things as they happen. War may be
glorious in its fruits and perhaps noble in its aims,
but it is cruel and horrible, and to gain a picture
of what it is it must be made so. There is nothing else to do but to treat it as reality—a grim, dreadful reality, not to be misunderstood.

Scarcely had Brooks been taken below, when this
fact was forced again on Perry's mind. Yarnell was
once more on deck. His head was swathed in red-
stained bandages.

"Can you let me have more men for the forward
guns?" he asked.

"You'll have to ask the surgeon for some of his
assistants. Tell him I sent you," was Perry's reply.

Yarnell disappeared. In a minute he returned, followed by two young lads fresh from their ghastly work
below. In five minutes Yarnell again stood before
Perry by the mast. His clothes were torn and he
reeled a little on his feet. *He had been wounded
the fourth time!*

"Those men have all been killed," he said.
"Let me have some more; we must keep that gun
a-going."

"I have no more men to give you," Perry answered quietly.

Yarnell saluted, and tottered forward to his post.

The roar of discharges now sounded in all directions, for the Lawrence had drifted within half pistol-shot of the vessels of the fleet that surrounded her. It looked as if the combat could be sustained no longer. Purser Hamilton, who had been serving at a gun and was shot through the body, was taken below by two slightly wounded men.

If the scene on deck was frightful, what must it have been down in that close, smoke-filled cockpit, crowded with wounded men, who lay in moaning huddles everywhere! Surgeon Usher Parsons was left all alone at his work. The cockpit was above the water line. Hamilton was placed beside the dying Brooks, and turned and spoke to him. The latter asked for Perry. The pain had left him now, and he spoke calmly and collectedly.

" If Perry's life is saved, he'll win us out of this," he said.

Hamilton was about to answer him, when something occurred so frightful and so unexpected that all thoughts were driven from his mind. Midshipman Henry Laub was on the table, having a ghastly wound in the shoulder dressed by the surgeon. With a crash a solid shot came through the side of the vessel and killed him where he lay. A Narragansett Indian who sat leaning against one of the timbers was hurled by this same shot across the narrow space, and fell dead among a pile of wounded.

And just at this moment the brave Brooks breathed his last.

Up on deck there was scarcely a score of men uninjured. Perry looked about him and saw that every officer was wounded with the exception of himself and his little brother. Near by stood Midshipman Dulancy Forrest, who was nursing a bruised arm. A shot came in through an open port, glanced, struck the mast, and glanced again. Its force was almost spent, but it caught the midshipman full in the chest, and down he went. Perry bent over him.

" Are you badly hurt, lad? " he asked anxiously.

The boy struggled to his feet; the breath was almost knocked out of his body.

" Not much, sir," he gasped, and then, thrusting his hand inside his waistcoat, he extricated something —it was the spent shot that had struck him!

" This is my ball, I think, sir," he went on, and calmly slipped it into his breeches pocket.

It is a strange thing that in moments of great excitement men take unusual happenings casually. There was no bravado in young Forrest's speech; he just expressed a thought that came into his mind. It was as simply done as it was simply said.

Joy now came into Perry's heart. Looking over the shattered bulwarks, he saw that a slight breeze had sprung up, and that before it the fleet was coming down to help him, the Niagara leading and

"If a victory is to be gained, I'll gain it."

(From an engraving by F. Phillibrown after the painting by W. H. Powell.)

the gunboats trailing yet a long way astern of her.
It had been almost two hours that he had been
fighting single-handed. And now help was coming
to him. He saw a chance also of taking advantage
of the wind and creeping away from the two vessels
that were harassing him most. Oh, if he could but
make sail! Turning to Forrest, he ordered him to
ask the surgeon to come up on deck. Usher Parsons appeared. Perry spoke a few quick words to
him, and he went below again.

"Is there any man here," he cried, when he had
reached the cockpit, "that is able to haul a rope?
If so, Captain Perry would like to see him on deck."

Five men, weak and gory, crawled out on hands
and knees and went up the ladder. During all this
time, although his heart was bleeding with anguish
at the spectacle of his brave lads torn to pieces,
Perry had made no outward sign of fear or grief.
But something occurred that forced a cry from him.
A ball striking in the bulwarks dislodged one of
the hammocks, which in its flight struck Midshipman
Perry in the chest, bowling him over like a nine-
pin. The commander raised him from the deck, and
then, to his joy, found that the lad was not even
stunned. Looking again across the water, he saw
that the Niagara, although nearer, was not coming
on fast enough. An idea seized him.

"Lower away that motto flag from the main-

mast!" he shouted, and hurriedly he ran to the taffrail and looked over. A little yawl that had been
towing astern was still floating there, with her oars in

Sword worn by
Com. Perry
at the battle of
Lake Erie.

her, as yet uninjured. He ran forward,
and found Yarnell leaning against the heel
of the bowsprit.

"Have you any men able to pull an
oar?" he asked the lieutenant.

Yarnell drew himself erect and looked
back at what was left of the crew. Only
nine men were unwounded.

"What are you going to do, sir?"
Yarnell asked.

"I am going to transfer my flag to
the Niagara," was Perry's quick reply.
"I'll fetch him up."

The little boat was brought alongside. The British, seeing the motto flag
come down from the masthead, slack-
ened in their fire. Four of the able-
bodied men slid down into the little boat.
Perry wrapped the motto flag around
his arm, and then he turned to Yarnell
again:

"I leave you in command of the ship,
sir."

"Very good, sir," the lieutenant replied, saluting; "I shall do my best."

They say that it has been done before. Historians tell us that in the battle of Solebay the Duke of York shifted his flag; and in the battle of the Texel, in 1673, the British Admiral Sprague shifted his flag twice, and was drowned in attempting to shift it a third time. The great Dutchman Van Tromp, in this same action, transferred his flag also. But precedent does not detract in the least from valorous deeds. When the British saw the big flag come down from the masthead they set up a most tremendous cheering, thinking that at last their dogged adversary had given up; but when they saw the little rowboat speed out from the enveloping cloud of smoke, they opened fire again, directing their batteries and their musketry at her.

Perry stood erect in the stern, the flag fluttering about him. Charges of grape spattered across the bow and stern. Round shot clipped the water but a few feet away, dashing the spray into the faces of the men bending at the oars. Two of the men in the sternsheets absolutely pulled their commander down from his exposed position, and all unharmed they swept in under the counter of the Niagara, whose cheering crew had been watching them. As Perry gained the deck he turned back and looked at the Lawrence, and as he did so the charnel ship with her crew of five hauled down her flag that had been flying at the peak. She could fight no more.

CHAPTER VIII.

ELLIOT grasped Perry's hand.

"Thank God, you're safe, sir!" he said. "But what a noble fight you made of it!"

"There are but few of my brave men left," Perry returned, "but very few of them. Let us take all the advantage of this breeze we can. Order close action. Bend on this flag to the color halyards, and hoist it to the masthead."

Proudly the emblem rose and tossed out to the air. No ship could surrender with those immortal words flying above her.

Elliot spoke quickly again as the commander almost groaned at seeing that the gunboats were out of striking distance.

"Grant me permission, sir," he said, "and I will go back in a boat and try to hurry them along."

No sooner was it asked than granted, and Elliot, as his superior had done, set out to bring the gunboats into action. He used the same boat that had brought Perry from the Lawrence.

The Englishmen, who were cheering again after the flagship had lowered her ensign, soon gave over, for out of the smoke that was drifting down toward the Yankee fleet came the Niagara, with Perry in command. It was no half-crippled, shattered hulk they had to face. Straight for their line the brig bore on. After her came the Somers, the Scorpion, and the smaller vessels, working their sweeps, and the men shouting as they redoubled their efforts to be up with their leader. It seemed as if every one was given giants' strength. The spectators on shore, who had been watching the action in great suspense, began tossing their hats into the air.

The presence of the commodore on board the Niagara stirred her crew to cheers.

" We are all right now! " exclaimed a grizzled old veteran who had followed deep water since he was old enough to lift an oar—" we're all right now, and the old man brought the breeze with him! Soon we'll have the little barkers talking." He slapped the breech of the gun playfully. The captain of a ship is always called the " old man " by his crew, a term of half endearment. There was no disrespect meant by the old sailor, for at that very moment he would have laid down his life for the tall young figure on the quarter-deck.

Perry's eyes were sparkling, but he gave his orders in the low, even tones that a sailor man knows and

6

recognizes so well, as those of one who is a master of himself and a leader of others.

"See!" suddenly exclaimed young Midshipman Perry, looking over his shoulder at his brother and pointing out across the water. Perry stooped and looked beneath the curving sweep of the foresail, and a smile crossed his face.

"Look at that brave fellow Yarnell!" he said proudly to one of the officers standing near him. "See there! he has drifted away from the fleet and hoisted his flag again."

Sure enough, the Lawrence had her colors once more at the peak. Brave Yarnell! Weakened by his wounds and suffering intense pain, with a shipload of dead and dying men, no sooner had he perceived that the British did not intend to board him than with his own hands he raised the flag. How the words of Lawrence must have been imprinted upon the minds of the men of the Erie fleet! They had them on the motto flag, and they had them deeply written on their hearts.

Perhaps the immortal words were the only things that Yarnell could think of. "Don't give up the ship!" he kept repeating, and he had determined that while he lived that flag should wave.

"I was shipmate with Yarnell for three years," spoke one of the younger officers, "and once I quarrelled with him. He is a brave fellow. I

The Niagara's advance.

(From a contemporary engraving.)

"Commodore Perry, having a short time before left the Lawrence in a small boat, amid a tremendous fire from the British squadron, and hoisted his flag on board the Niagara. The Lawrence is seen at a distance disabled.

"Represents the position of the two fleets at the moment when the Niagara is pushing through the enemy's line, pouring her thunder upon them from both broadsides, and forcing them to surrender in succession to the American flag."—*Description on engraving.*

hope that we both are spared, that I may ask his
pardon."

But there was little time for conversation. There
was soon to be hot work indeed.

The English fleet had begun to maneuver, and
were heading this way and that in obedience to the
signals of their flagship. They were endeavoring to
get in line to receive the onslaught of the American
squadron. Perry left the quarter-deck and hurried to
the forecastle. They were almost within range, and
yet not a gun had been fired. The smoke of the previous action with the Lawrence had blown away, and
lay like a thin mist over the water to leeward. The
fickle wind again had shifted and caught some of the
English vessels all aback. The Niagara took advantage of it and bore up a little. Her broadside guns
covered the nearest English ships. The old sailor who
had spoken to his comrades when the commodore
had come on board almost groaned. He squinted
along the barrel of the long twelve-pounder and lowered the breech a little. Perry observed the motion.

"Have you the range there, Judson?" he called
out.

"Aye, aye, sir, that I have!" the old tar replied,
blushing that the commodore had remembered his
name. "I think I can cripple her, sir!"

The Queen Charlotte, whose crew were working
like ants endeavoring to bring her head around, was

gathering sternway. Just abaft her quarter was the
Detroit, and she also seemed in difficulties. A quick
glance told Perry that the forward starboard gun was
in position to do great damage, but there was not an
accent of excitement in his voice as he turned quickly.

"You may fire, Judson," he said; and scarcely had
he spoken when the forecastle was shrouded in smoke,
and at the roar of the gun every man looked to see
the effect of the shot.

Often and often has it been proved that defeat or
victory hinged upon one movement or one single
well-directed effort, and people term it "luck." Perhaps in some cases it may be, but, if so, good fortune
had squinted along the barrel of Judson's gun.

The ball carried away one of the stays, and crip-
pled some of the running rigging in such a manner
that the Queen Charlotte's fore-topsail went back
against the mast, and before the Detroit could get
out of the way the flagship had run afoul of her. They
ranged side by side, the stem of one lying close to
the stern of the other. The yards became twisted in
the shrouds, and the running gear that was let go
suddenly fouled so completely that soon they were
locked together and hopelessly entangled.

Now was the time for action. Perry hastened
back to the quarter-deck.

"Hold your fire! hold your fire!" he cried to the
impatient gunners who were waiting for the word.

"It was a good shot, Dan!" exclaimed one of the younger sailors to the old veteran.

"God is with us this day," put in a tall New-Englander. "He's fighting on our side."

Perry spoke a few words to the quartermaster at the wheel. Nearer and nearer the Niagara ranged. The blows of the axes in the hands of the men who were trying to separate the English vessels could be distinctly heard, and the voices of the officers urging them on. It almost seemed as if the Niagara would soon be afoul of the others, so close was she ranging. The thump of the handspikes on the deck as the men brought their guns to bear, and the flapping of the great maintopsails that had come back against the mast, added to the sounds that came from the English vessels. They were now but two points forward of the beam, and in another instant Perry had given the word.

No broadside that had been poured into the poor defenseless Lawrence had been as destructive as that that leaped from the Niagara's side. The crushing force of the heavy short-range guns was seen. Splinters flew and great gashes were ripped in the bow and stern of the Detroit and the Queen. Whole charges and grapeshot swept the crowded decks. It was one of those dreadful transformation scenes that have happened and always will happen in battle. The stricken ships shivered beneath the blows. The busy axes ceased. The shrieks and groans rose. A young officer who had been aloft fell heavily from the foretop to the deck. From a crowd of men on the forecastle

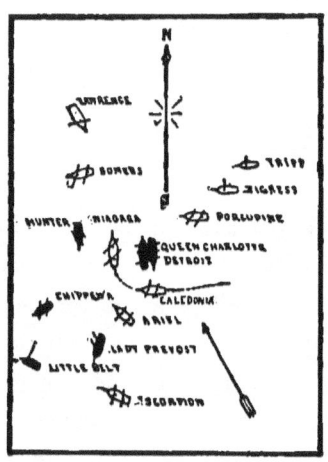

Diagram of the battle, No. 2.

only one or two managed to scramble to their feet, badly wounded. A grim look was on the faces of the Yankee gunners.

"That for the Lawrence!" exclaimed old Judson.

Perry had remained unmoved. He spoke a few quiet words to one of the lieutenants. The men sprang to the braces and heaved the yards around.

On the Niagara swept, heading for the Lady Provost, that lay but a short distance off to port. "Here come the little ones!" exclaimed one of the officers, pointing back over the taffrail. " Here's Turner in the Caledonia! "

The Yankee cheers filled the air as the smaller craft came into action. They followed close upon the heels of the Niagara, and as each one passed the English ships she let go her little broadside. Well were those guns served and aimed! Just as the Porcupine passed by there came a crash, and the mainmast of the Detroit fell, bringing down everything in its wake, and a few seconds afterward the mizzenmast of the Queen Charlotte fell also.

The port broadside of the Niagara now spoke in earnest, and the Lady Provost reeled from the shot that swept her from stern to bow. The little British gunboat Hunter was destined to be the next victim, but just as the gunners were training their pieces upon her a British officer in full uniform mounted the bulwarks. He waved a white flag at the end of a pikestaff, and at the same time down fluttered the English ensign.

" Cease firing! " came the order from the quarter-deck. But a few shots from any of the English vessels had reached the Niagara, although she had not escaped unscathed. A round shot from one of the bow guns of the English flagship had killed two men, and twenty-five of her crew had been wounded by splinters and musket balls.

As the haze of smoke cleared away, it was seen

that the two remaining Englishmen were doing their best to escape. They had crowded on all sail and were making off as fast as they could.

"There go the Chippewa and Little Belt!" Perry exclaimed; "but see, the Scorpion and the Trippe are hot after them!"

It was an exciting race to watch. There was plenty to do in clearing away the wreckage and looking after the dead and wounded, but every now and then the men would steal a glance at the fleeing vessels and their pursuers. Every minute the latter were gaining, and when it was perceived that they would soon head them the sailors on the Niagara and the rest of the fleet began to cheer again. "There the Scorpion speaks!" exclaimed an old sailor. "And the Trippe isn't far behind her!" put in another.

The captains of the Little Belt and the Chippewa saw the game was up, and, after the interchange of a few shots, down came their flags. The victory was complete. The power of the English upon the lakes had vanished. The borderland was safe!

Perry gazed out over the water as the smoke cleared away. He recognized all the importance of what had been accomplished. He realized that with one bound he had achieved fame, and yet well he knew at what cost it was and what a price his brave men had paid. Gazing off to the southward, he saw

The smaller vessels coming into action.

(From a contemporary engraving.)

the wreck of the Lawrence, and noticed again with a flush of pride that her flag was flying.

The stillness seemed uncanny after the furious clamor of the guns. The occasional groan of a wounded man, the sound of axes, and the voices of officers shouting orders alone broke the stillness. A thought crossed Perry's mind : By every right, the principal honor of the victory belonged to the tattered hulk that had so long borne the brunt of the battle alone! He turned to an officer who was standing close by him.

"Call away a boat," he said quietly, "and put me on board the Lawrence. I will receive the surrender there."

A feeble cheer greeted him as he reached the flagship's side. Wounded men crawled to the ports and weakly raised themselves at the rail. Tears filled the young commander's eyes as he stepped upon the deck. There had been no time to clear away the _débris_ and wreckage, nor even to take care and move all the wounded below. The heaps of slain, some frightfully mangled, crowded the deck. With the assistance of the crew of the boat that had rowed the commodore off, a shred of sail was made upon the foremast, but it was found impossible to gain steerage way, and the attempt was abandoned.

Lieutenant Yarnell and Surgeon Parsons had met Perry as he clambered over the side. "I have

come back to the old ship," said the young commander.

"Thank God, you have been saved to us!" exclaimed Yarnell.

Perry turned to him. "And I thank God, too,"
he said, "to find that you are living to share the victory. When I saw that you had hoisted your flag
again I knew that we would be successful."

At this moment a boat from the Caledonia came
alongside, and an officer reported. As he looked
about him he turned pale. The rest of the fleet had
not known how dreadful had been the struggle that
the Lawrence had gone through. "Are you going to
receive the surrender here, sir?" he asked, saluting.

"I am," was Perry's reply. "Will you pass the
word to the captured vessels?"

The officer hastened to his boat. It was with a
sigh of relief that he put off from the side. The ship
was full of the groans that came from the crowded
cockpit. Usher Parsons returned below to his work.
Never could that sight leave the minds of any one
who witnessed it. Overhead the sky was blue and
clear, all the smoke had disappeared, and over the
dimpled waters of the lake the vessels floated, huddled near to one another. It was like the lull and
stillness that follow a tremendous storm. Perry
walked to the rail. The greatest day of his life had
come and passed. The thoughts that filled his mind

crowded one upon another in quick succession, but
one was uppermost. It was not a vainglorious ex-
ultation, but a thankfulness for deliverance from danger and a wide, great love for the men who had shared
it with him and who had suffered and died for their
country's sake.

But now the whole fleet was drifting down nearer
and nearer, and soon boats put off from the English
vessels, and in the stern sheets sat officers bearing
their side arms in their hands. Never could they forget the sight that greeted them as they came to the
Lawrence's deck. She was filled with the groans of
the wounded below, above which sounded the mournful wailing of a little dog confined somewhere in the
hold. A group of silent men watched the officers come
on board. Near the wheel stood Perry. His pale
face was set, but with no look of triumph or elation.
His arms were folded, and as each officer approached
and offered his sword in token of submission, the hero
of Erie bowed slightly.

" I request that you will keep your sword, sir,"
he said to each. " It has been bravely used and worn."

The ceremony was short, for there was much to
be done. The English officers were anxious to get
away; even a prison would be better than being on
board that charnel ship. Some were so overcome that
they shut their eyes, and one commander, a man of
experience and used to war's dreadful necessities, stag-

gered weakly to the side. He supported himself against the bulwarks. It is safe to state that never before nor since had such terrible slaughter taken place on board a ship of any navy. But as the news of the victory was spreading below in the crowded cockpit, all the wounded had displayed signs of gratification; and when the surgeon had brought the word that all the enemy had struck, the brave fellows tried to raise their voices in response. Years afterward, when Usher Parsons was an old man, he spoke as follows: "The idea that Perry was safe seemed to reconcile every man to his own suffering, but I can never forget the scene. The deck was slippery with blood, and strewed with the bodies of more than twenty officers and men, some of whom had sat at table with us at our last meal, and the ship resounded with the groans of the wounded. Those of us who were spared and able to walk met him at the gangway to welcome him on board, but the salutation was a silent one—no one could utter but a word. And now the British officers arrived, one from each vessel, to tender their submission and with it their swords. I remember as they approached they picked their way among the wreck and carnage, extending the hilts of their side arms toward Perry, tendering them for his acceptance. With a dignified and solemn air, and in a low tone of voice, he requested them to retain their side arms, inquired in deep concern for Commodore Barclay and the wounded officers, tendering them every comfort his ship afforded, and expressing his regret that he had not a spare medical officer to send them; that he had only one on duty for the fleet, and that one had his hands full."

As soon as the last British officer left the Lawrence, Perry called young Midshipman Forrest to him. It was important that the news of this victory should reach the ears of the general commanding the American troops on shore as soon as possible. To be the bearer of such a dispatch was a coveted honor, and Perry had not chosen amiss in thus selecting and rewarding a lad who had displayed such courage and coolness in action.

Removing his heavy hat and placing it on his knee, Perry searched through his pockets for some paper on which to write the message. He found nothing but an old letter. Tearing off the back, he hastily scribbled the following note—one that has become historic, and that will always live as a model of moderate and humble expression:

U. S. BRIG NIAGARA, OFF THE WESTERN SISTER,
HEAD OF LAKE ERIE,
September 10, 1813, at 4 P. M.

"DEAR GENERAL: We have met the enemy and they are ours. Two ships, two brigs, one schooner, and one sloop.

"Yours, with great respect and esteem,

"O. H. PERRY."

Young Forrest took this note and started in a small boat for the shore. It was dead calm now on the lake, and the moon rose early. It looked down upon a strange scene. Perry had wisely determined, before sailing back to harbor, to clear away as much of the wreckage and signs of the carnage as possible. The dead were made ready for burial in the waters of the lake, and, after a short service, English and American were sent off together, each wrapped in a sailor's shroud of a hammock with a round shot at his heels. The dead officers were placed in roughly constructed coffins to be brought ashore for more ceremonious burial.

But let us look at the reports of the losses sustained by both sides during this action: The Lawrence flagship had twenty-two killed and sixty-one wounded; the Niagara, two killed and twenty-five wounded; the Scorpion, two killed; the Ariel, one killed and three wounded; the Caledonia, three wounded; the Somers, two wounded; the Trippe, two wounded—in all, twenty-seven were killed outright and ninety-six were wounded, which foots up to a total of one hundred and twenty-three. When we subtract from this the loss sustained on board the Lawrence, we perceive how slight were the injuries of the others, and what a part she bore in the action.

The British loss was even greater in the aggregate than the American, being forty-one killed and

ninety-four wounded, a total of one hundred and thirty-five. All the unwounded prisoners were placed on board the Porcupine and were landed at Cannon River.

Perry endeared himself to the foe by the manner in which he personally superintended arranging for the care of the wounded and the comfort of the prisoners. Brave Commodore Barclay had kept on deck throughout the engagement, but he had suffered severely. His right arm had been lost years before while fighting under Nelson, and the sleeve was pinned across his chest. In the early part of the action he had been wounded in the thigh, and shortly afterward by a musket ball in the left shoulder, that rendered him absolutely incapable of taking care of himself. He could scarcely stand, and now both arms were useless. But the brave man's spirit kept him going. His indomitable will did not fail him. Perry had given up his own cabin to the wounded leader, and from the very first displayed a keen desire to do anything in his power to alleviate his sufferings. On the 12th, after the fleet had landed the wounded, there was held a ceremony that is a tradition in Put-in-Bay, and there is yet living in Detroit a man who remembers having witnessed it as a boy. Thus often are we linked back by one life to affairs and doings that appear ancient history almost, or at least are claimed by the misty long ago. The burial of the officers must have

been a scene long to be remembered. Preceded by
a band of music playing a funeral march came the
funeral *cortège*, bearing the six coffins containing the
bodies of three American and three British officers:
Midshipman Henry Laub, Midshipman John Clark,
and the gallant Lieutenant Brooks, whose death we
have recorded; Captain Finnis and Lieutenant Stokes
of the Queen Charlotte, and Lieutenant Garland of the
Detroit. Before the landing had been made there had
been a procession of boats, rowing minute strokes,
and, as an eyewitness describes it, "the slow and regular motion of the oars, striking in exact time with the
notes of the solemn dirge, the mournful waving of
flags, and the sound of minute guns from the ships
presented a striking contrast to the scene of two days
before, when both the living and the dead, now forming in this solemn and fraternal train, were engaged in
fierce and bloody strife."

As they marched to the place of burial the crews
of both fleets followed the mourning officers, and when
they ranged about the graves there was to be seen a
peculiar sight. Master-Commandant Perry, the hero
of Erie, stood there, supporting with his arm the
wounded and shattered figure of Commodore Barclay,
who leaned heavily against him. The brave officer
had insisted upon attending the ceremony, and after
it was all over he was taken to Perry's quarters, where
the latter waited upon him personally, and sat by his

bedside half the night. War is a dreadful thing, but it does not necessarily mean a hatred of an honest enemy. Often admiration for the generosity or bravery of an adversary calls up feelings akin to love and affection.

CHAPTER IX.

AFTER a battle has been fought there come to
light many incidents and occurrences that are not
noticed during the heat of action, and sometimes they
escape the attention of even the careful historian.
Little details that are of great interest can not be
spoken of in describing great effects, but at the same
time they should not be allowed to pass by unno-
ticed, although their consequences are of not much
moment.

When the Niagara had delivered her broadside at
the Lady Provost, it had swept the decks and so dis-
heartened the crew that all had run below—all but
one man, dressed in the uniform of a lieutenant, and,
strange to say, he stood there calmly in the compan-
ion way, with his chin resting on his hand, gazing
fixedly at the Niagara as she passed. What it meant
no one knew at the time, but afterward it was ascertained that he was Lieutenant Buchan, and that a
wound in the head from a musket ball had deranged
his mind. Thus he had stood there utterly uncon-

scious that he was in danger and oblivious to his surroundings.

The English had enlisted into their service for this battle some Indian warriors belonging to the tribes that they had hired to make a border warfare against the Americans, but broadside to broadside was not their style of fighting. After the engagement had begun, they had skulked like the redskins that they were, and had hidden in the depths of the vessel's hold.

Years afterward there was started a newspaper controversy that developed great bitterness between the personal friends of Master-Commandant Elliot and those of Perry.

But the conduct of the hero of Erie was dignified, and he certainly did not begin the affair, as he laid no charge against his brother officer and certainly did him full justice in his detailed report of the engagement to the Secretary of the Navy. In fact, his report is of such great interest and is so just and fair that it may be best to give it space here.

Perry writes as follows in regard to the conduct of his officers: " Lieutenant Yarnell, although several times wounded, refused to quit the deck. Midshipman Forrest and Sailing-Master Taylor were of great assistance to me. I have great pain in reporting the death of Lieutenant John Brooks, of the marines, Midshipman Henry Laub, of the Lawrence, and John Clark, of the Scorpion; they were valuable and promising officers. Samuel Hambleton, purser, who volunteered his services on deck, was severely wounded late in the action. Midshipman Thomas Claxton and Augustus Swartwout, of the Lawrence, were severely wounded. Lieutenants Smith and John J. Edwards and Midshipman Nelson Webster, of the Niagara, behaved in a very handsome manner. Captain Brevoort, of the army, who acted as a volunteer marine in the Niagara, is an excellent and brave officer, and did great execution with his musketry. Lieutenant Turner, of the Caledonia, brought that vessel into action in a most able manner, and is an officer who in all situations may be relied on. The Ariel, Lieutenant Packett, and the Scorpion, Sailing-Master Champlin, were enabled to get into action early, and were of great service. Master-Commandant Elliot spoke in the highest terms of Humphry Magrath, purser, who had been dispatched in a boat on service previously to getting on board the Niagara, and, being a seaman, had rendered essential service since the action by taking charge of one of the prizes. Of Master-Commandant Elliot, already so well known to the Government, it would be almost superfluous to speak. In this action he evinced his characteristic bravery and judgment."

Besides the honor which was gained by all who had any connection with the battle of the lakes, substantial rewards were also reaped. Gold medals were awarded to Perry and Elliot, silver medals to each of the commissioned officers, and silver medals also to the nearest male relatives of Lieutenant Brooks, and to the nearest relatives of Midshipman Henry Laub, Thomas Claxton, and John Clark were given swords. To all the officers, seamen, and marines was awarded an extra three months' pay, in addition to which Congress voted $225,000 prize money to be divided among the victorious crews.

Commodore Chauncey, who, although not actually in action, was the chief in command on the lakes, received $12,750; Perry and Elliot $7,150 each, but Congress supplemented this by an additional $5,000 to Perry. Each commander of a gunboat, sailing master, lieutenant, and lieutenant of marines received $2,295; midshipmen, $811; petty officers, $447; marines and sailors, $209 apiece.

But now let us return to the doings of Commodore Perry — the "commodore" by courtesy, for he still bore only the rank of master commandant.

Strange to say, his next duty was on land, where he fought as a volunteer and aid-de-camp to General Harrison.

Although the British had lost all their vessels in the lakes, they were still in great force on the Canadian shore, and until they had been dislodged or their organization partially broken the American power could not be firmly established.

The English prisoners were landed at Sandusky and hurried on to Chillicothe, Ohio, and, as soon as the ships could be placed in readiness, the American troops were embarked for the contemplated attack upon Malden.

On the 22d of September Commodore Perry landed twelve hundred infantry on a small island about twelve miles from the English stronghold, and the next day they were embarked and landed upon the Canadian shore, near the town of Amherstburg, which had been evacuated, and was immediately taken possession of. It was at once ascertained that the English General Proctor had decided upon retreat. He had burned the fort at Malden, the barracks, the navy yard, and the public storehouses, and had started up country with all his forces.

General Harrison pressed on in pursuit. Proctor was heading for the river Thames, which empties into Lake St. Clair, about twenty-five miles above Detroit.

On the 2d of October Perry volunteered to become an aid on General Harrison's staff, and started with the army from the town of Sandwich close upon Proctor's heels. The American army was composed of but one hundred and forty regulars, and amounted in the aggregate to not more than thirty-five hundred men. They included a mounted regiment, under

command of the brave Colonel Johnson, who had made
a name for himself in the wars with the Indians, and
the Kentucky troops, in command of Governor Shelby,
a veteran of the war of the Revolution, who, though
well over sixty, had all the strength, dash, and courage of his early days.

As they approached the river Thames, the path
of the English forces could be distinctly noticed.
They had attempted to destroy everything which
might help to support the pursuing forces, and houses
and granaries and barns were left in smoking ruins.
Even the scanty crops of grain that had been gathered in the fields had been destroyed.

On the morning of the 3d the banks of the Thames
were reached, and the army crossed unmolested over
a rickety old bridge which Proctor had set fire to,
but which had not been wholly destroyed. But there
were before General Harrison the three branches of
the river, all deep and rapid streams, and it was not
expected that they would pass them without meeting
some of the enemy.

Speed in pursuit makes up for numbers, and, without waiting to camp or for the baggage to arrive
(this had been brought partly around by boat), Harrison pushed ahead with the mounted detachments,
galloping as fast as the horses could go over the rough
and uneven country.

Perry, who had changed his calling from that of

the seaman to that of a cavalryman, had been fortunate enough to secure a good horse that had been
left behind at Amherstburg, possibly by one of the
English officers.

It was hard to tell when they would meet the rear
guard of the enemy. At any point in the valleys or
hills they might be ambushed.

Harrison did not expect to take the bridges without resistance. At one o'clock in the afternoon,
Perry, who was riding in advance with one of the
lieutenants, came over the brow of a steep hill, and
there below him saw a small force of infantry de-
ployed across the road at the entrance to the first
bridge. Some men were working with axes and ex-
temporized crowbars, trying to tear up the planks
and undermine the bridge seats. Without waiting
to ascertain whether Proctor's whole army was drawn
up on the other side of the tall bushes and trees, Harrison called for a charge, and, with him and Perry at
the head, the mounted regiment swept down. The
Englishmen were taken by surprise. Scarcely a shot
was fired, and all those who did not have time to run
across were captured. Among them were a lieutenant of dragoons, eleven privates of his regiment, and
some infantry.

Onward they pressed across the dividing land that
rose gradually between the valleys of the branches
of the stream. The same condition of affairs was

found to exist at the next bridge, although the work of destruction had progressed somewhat more. The farther end of it was in flames, and but few of the logs that served for planking remained, but without hesitancy the mounted force swept down. One or two of the troopers sustained falls by reason of their horses' legs going through the woodwork, but with a cheer they rushed bravely across, and it was but the work of a few minutes to extinguish the flames.

Leaving a small guard at the entrance, Harrison pressed on; but, finding that he could not reach the North Fork until nightfall, he returned and placed Perry in charge of repairing the bridge, after which he hastened back to facilitate the forward movement of the rest of the army. Late that night the baggage arrived, coming up the river by boat, and there camp was built and a strong guard was established.

As we have mentioned before, the British on the northwestern frontier had engaged the services of the Canadian Indian troops, and also of some of the nations who for a long time had been at war with the New York, the Ohio, and the Kentucky frontiersmen. These Indians were not bad fighters, and on this occasion they had for their leader the celebrated chief Tecumseh, who, although he was feared by his enemies, the American whites, bore a reputation for honesty and bravery second to none of the great chieftains who had given so much trouble.

When the last bridge was found, instead of it being
protected by a line of English troops, the only force
that showed itself was a band of several hundred Indians, who stood without intrenchments on the farther side. They were evidently prepared to dispute
the passage of the American forces, and to obstruct
the repairing of the bridge. They were well armed,
and it seemed that there would be a large sacrifice of
life in case a charge was ordered. Perry was sent back
to the rear with instructions to bring up two six-
pounders. It was no easy work to get them through
the woods and to keep them from sinking hub-deep
in the soft, rain-soaked roads, but he managed to
bring them to the front, and, after a few well-directed
shots, the Indians retired. In two hours the bridge
was repaired, and the troops marched across.

There was a little house on the hill that had been
occupied by a Canadian settler. At first nothing
amiss was noticed, but suddenly one of the younger
officers pointed out that smoke was coming from the
open windows, and, before a movement could be
made, it was seen that the upper story was in flames.
It was so near the river that water could be pro-
cured without great difficulty, and the fire was ex-
tinguished. The British had left in this house a quan-
tity of gunpowder and muskets, all of which were welcome trophies of war.

Away up the river above the trees a thin column

of smoke was seen ascending the air, and when some of the Americans had skirted the river bank, it was found that one of the British vessels, probably from Malden, had been towed and worked up there and at the last moment had been fired. All this proved that the enemy were not far away, and that soon they would be forced to turn and fight.

About four miles above where the first vessel was seen, two more were afterward found in flames. At the top of a large hill a big building was discovered toward evening burning fiercely. Although every effort was made to get at the contents and subdue the fire, it had progressed so far that the only property saved were two mounted twenty-four-pounders and a few shot and shell.

At this place, which was known as the Distillery, the troops camped that night, and before daybreak next morning they were again in motion, and by three o'clock one of the scouts announced to General Harrison that the enemy had halted and were preparing to meet them. It was without doubt Proctor's intention to reach this very point, and there to make his stand. He had not chosen it haphazard, nor had he been forced to take it. With military judgment and forethought he recognized the advantages of the position. A large and almost impassable swamp followed the bend of the river for several miles. The hilltop was covered with a great forest of beech trees, almost clear of underbrush, and the other side swept down into a tangle of tamarack and stunted pine.

The road by which the Americans had been approaching ran through the forest near to the bank of the stream, or, better, the juncture of the swamp. All the artillery had been placed to guard the open approach, the Indian auxiliaries had been massed in the swamp, and a line of well-intrenched infantrymen filled the hillsides among the pines.

In Harrison's report he gives great credit to Perry for suggestions, and proves that the hero of Erie, besides possessing nautical skill, could boast of no little military ability. The accounts of the little battle that followed are not known to many readers of American history, but yet it deserves mention, not only because of its real importance, but because of the doings of the backwoodsmen who formed the majority of the forces.

As they formed in order of battle, the brigade under command of General Trotter took the front line, with his right upon the road and his left upon the swamp. Next came General Desha's division, formed in two lines to the left. Less than two hundred yards in the rear of Trotter's brigade came that of General King, while one brigade was held back as a reserve force in the rear. Each brigade numbered nearly five hundred men. It was the first intention

to try to turn the flank that the Indians held, and to
push them in from the right; but, owing to the swampi-
ness of the ground and the denseness of the foliage,
the horses could not be used, and it was seen that
the men as they came across the open space would
find themselves exposed to a withering fire.

It seemed that Proctor had guarded at every point,
but he did not count upon certain qualities which have
shown themselves in the character of the American
soldier when hard pressed or thwarted. It can best
be described by the word "initiative"—an unhesi-
tating and simultaneous action arising from the individual efforts of the men to relieve the situation. It
was always supposed that artillery sheltered by woods
was safe from a cavalry charge. In many a battle
have batteries of artillery been taken by a fierce onslaught of mounted men charging in the open, but
when protected by trees it had never happened. Of
course, the fierce weight of the attack would be
broken by dodging in and out among the trunks, and
the Englishmen's tactics prescribed no method of
getting around them.

However, the Kentucky riflemen (some of whom
were mounted) and all of the backwoods companies
that were on horseback were gathered on both sides
of the road that ran to the forest. At a given order
they were to join forces and go headlong to the artillery that was among the beeches at the top of the

hill. As the forward movement took place, firing began on both left and right, and then, as the head of the column appeared in the road, the artillery opened up. At first the horsemen were thrown into confusion, but suddenly a strong, clear voice rang out:

" Now, lads, up and at them before they can get in another broadside! "

Perry had left Harrison's side, and his quick eye had seen the opportunity. The English, shrouded in their own smoke, and knowing that it would take some time for the Americans to cross the ground on foot, and doubting that they would dare to do so, did not see the band of horsemen gallop into the open. They did not hear the order to charge, and the first thing they knew mounted men were all around them in the woods. In fact, the guns were captured and the English line broken in less than two minutes' actual time, for the mounted infantry rode through them, wheeled and turned, and fired again, and in those two minutes the battle was won. Strange to say, not a single American horseman was killed, and but three were wounded!

The Indians, however, were making a good fight of it upon the American left, and here the American advance was checked; but the same riflemen who had captured the batteries, swinging off toward the swamp, got in on the higher ground behind it, and now Tecum-

seh's men found themselves between two fires. It was more than flesh and blood could stand, and they broke and retreated in all directions. The day was won.

Six hundred prisoners of the British regulars surrendered, twelve were killed, and twenty-two wounded. The Indians lost thirty-three dead, whose bodies were found in the swamp and the surrounding hillsides. Six brass field pieces were taken, and, strange to say, three were discovered to be trophies of the Revolutionary War, and they were the same ones that had been surrendered to the British by General Hull at Detroit. Originally they had been taken from the British at Saratoga and Yorktown some thirty years before!

Almost all of the small arms that were captured had also previously belonged to the Americans, and had been taken at Detroit, Frenchtown, or one of the skirmishes along the Miami.

As a group of officers rode over the field of battle, a sergeant approached and, saluting, spoke a few words to General Harrison.

"Are you sure that it is he, my man?" said the general in reply to the sergeant's words.

"I know him well by sight, sir," was the answer. "He lies just beyond the farther hill."

Riding over in that direction, they found a number of men surrounding a figure on the ground. It was that of the brave Indian Tecumseh. At the time of his death he bore a commission as brigadier general in the English army, and his name was one to conjure with among the Indian tribes. Although he hated the United States, his method of conducting war had always been that of a high-minded leader. He had been more anxious than the English for the action, and previous to it he had berated Proctor for showing a disposition to retreat.

In making his report, Harrison did not forget to mention the value of the services of his voluntary aid. He writes of Perry as follows:

"Commodore Perry assisted me in forming the troops for action, and his appearance cheered and animated every breast."

CHAPTER X.

It happened that news of the victory on the lakes came to the people at large when they were much depressed and exceedingly down-hearted over the way things had been going with the army on the frontier. It needed just such news to create a new spirit and revive the public zeal. A contemporary wrote, in the strange old style to which writers of the early part of the century were prone:

" No wonder this victory communicates a ray of joy to every American bosom. It occasioned through the country every visible testimonial of public rejoicing. In all of our principal cities illuminations took place, accompanied with other demonstrations of joy, admiration, and gratitude. All felt the animating influence of the victory so splendid in its character and so important in its consequences. All participated in the general joy. The merchant laid aside his ledger, the mechanic the implements of his trade, the man of business suspended his exertions, the laborer his toil, and the speculator forgot his golden dreams for a moment, all uniting in one common demonstration of joy and gratitude."

Which all goes to prove that Perry, like Admiral Dewey in our day, found himself a much-admired individual.

Congress and the people at large showed their approbation in every possible way. Besides the money which had been voted him, he was presented with numerous tokens and honorable mementos. His journey through the country wherever he went was an ovation. It is a wonder that he ever survived the number of dinners and receptions where the lists of toasts were as long as your arm.

But what had pleased Perry most was undoubtedly his promotion to the rank of captain, to date from the day of his victory.

A strange little side light upon the character of the young commander is shown by the fact that after his long journey from the lakes to Newport, R. I., he still had kept by him the four brave men who had rowed his boat out from the shattered Lawrence to the Niagara. Wherever he went they accompanied him, a self-constituted guard of honor.

But an idle life was not to the young captain's liking, and certainly that at Newport was not conducive to happiness in Perry's eyes. What he needed and craved was activity and a chance for the exercise of his commanding powers, and so early in January, 1814, he

started overland for Washington. We, who travel so
easily and luxuriously in our express trains, have no
idea of the tediousness and length of such a journey
during the older times. Think of sometimes being
three or four days from Boston to New York, and just
as long from that city to Washington!

On the 11th he arrived in New York, and a splendid
entertainment was given him in Tammany Hall (which
was very different from the Tammany Hall nowadays).
Strange to say, just at this time politics had begun to
creep into interstate transactions. Many people in
New England, and especially those who had interests
at Boston, had bitterly opposed the declaration of hos-
tilities against Great Britain, and it was not until a number of our victories at sea had begun to restore confidence that these birds of ill-omen ceased their croaking.
In New York, which was an important center of parti-
sanship, there were many factions, and there were many
political parties on the verge of formation that might
cause destruction to the national policy. When Perry
rose to respond to the speech of welcome, he looked
down the large hall, and without making any references
to the condition of affairs or to the reason of his being
there, in a few simple words he pledged "the union of
the States." He spoke of the necessity of their standing together. It often requires but a few words at the
right time to weld what might become separate and an-
tagonistic sections strongly together. It was like the

well-directed and skillful blows of the hammer that forge the two ends of a band of steel.

A tumultuous applause greeted his little speech, and afterward it was said that his words had done more good than all the outpourings of the press.

There is but the account of one more entertainment that was given in his honor, and we will resume the more interesting part of his life.

Baltimore is a town always renowned for its hospitality. They did not do things by halves in those days, and on the 1st of February an entertainment was given to Perry that was so unusual that it attracted great attention throughout the country, and accounts of it were copied from one paper to another. What it was really like, in view of the manner in which such a thing could be done nowadays, with electric lights, complicated mechanisms, and all that, we can not judge, so perhaps it is well to quote directly from a contemporary newspaper, Niles's Register, that was published in Baltimore:

" On Tuesday, Commodore Perry was entertained at Barney's Fountain Inn in a manner that we beg to be indulged in communicating and recording, for reasons that may be urged hereafter." (The reasons that the editor urges are that the whole affair is a nation's business.) Then he goes on, after mentioning some of the people who were present:

" At the head of a large room was a large transparent

painting, reaching almost across the hall, representing the battle of Erie. The accomplished artist had happily seized that moment, when Commodore Perry, 'at forty-five minutes past two, having thrown out the signal for close action,' bore up in the Niagara and passed ahead of their two ships and a brig, giving a raking fire to them from the starboard guns, and to a large schooner and sloop from the larboard side at half-pistol-shot distance. The smaller vessels having at this time got within grape and canister distance, under the direction of Captain Elliot, and keeping up a well-directed fire, the two ships, a brig, and a schooner surrendered, a schooner and a sloop making a vain attempt to escape.

"The painting was finely executed, and its effect was charming. At the head of the tables was the representation of a stern of a ship, labeled 'Niagara,' on which, as on the quarter-deck, were placed the president of the day, Edward Johnson, Esq., with the hero, Commodores Lewis and Barney, and Captains Spence and Ridgely, of the U. S. Navy, and other invited guests. In front of these rose, as in a great column, a bundle of eighteen arrows, braced together by massy bands, on which were inscribed the names of Hull, Jones, Decatur, Bainbridge, Lawrence, Ludlow, Burrows, Allen, and Perry, in large letters of gold. From the center of the arrows rose a topgallant mast and yard, bearing a flag on which was inscribed the mem-

orable dispatch, 'We have met the enemy and they
are ours.' The pedestal was ornamented with naval
emblems and wreaths. Over the whole was suspended
the American eagle, bearing in his beak a scroll let-
tered 'A nation's gratitude the hero's best reward.'
This effigy was so managed that, with outstretched
wings, it passed, occasionally, over the company. . . .
The windows of the room were elegantly curtained
with the 'striped bunting' spangled with stars, and
whichever way the eye turned it fell on some object
to delight the sense and gratify the patriotic enthusi-
asm that overflowed every bosom. The music gallery
was filled with gentlemen amateurs, and their excellent performances added not a little to embellish and
adorn the whole.

"The vice-presidents were Joseph H. Nicholson,
Esq., Captain Samuel Sterett, Major Isaac McKim,
Colonel James Biays, Captain George Stiles, and
Major Thomas Tenant; and the company, amounting
to between two and three hundred gentlemen, sat
down to dinner a little before five o'clock. Dignified
order, with heartfelt animation and joy, held uninter-
rupted sway until nine in the evening, when the company broke up, and each went home rejoicing that he
had seen that day, so honorable to all concerned in the
tribute of gratitude to the hero of Erie.

"As the several toasts were announced, the music
struck up a patriotic air. But when this was repeated

by the vice-president, the company directed its attention in silence toward the musicians, wondering why
they did not play. Suddenly the roll of a drum, as if
first at a great distance, was heard behind the trans-
parency, and every eye was turned that way. The roll
grew louder and louder, and having reached its entire
force, down came the British flag from the enemy's ships
in the foreground of the picture; then the band struck
up 'Yankee Doodle,' and the British flag was hoisted
under the American ensign. Very few of the company
were aware of this; it is folly to attempt to describe the
feelings it excited."

Boston also honored the hero of Erie by presenting
him with a set of silver service, a sword, and the free-
dom of the city. Besides this, he received many gifts
of plate from private individuals.

On the 30th of May Perry was once more in Newport. A strange state of affairs existed along the
American coasts and in the waters of the Sound. The
English had at their disposal at this time such an im-
mense fleet of vessels that there was hardly an inhabited
point on the American coast from which one could not
see a sail of the enemy almost every day or so. The
vessels of the American navy in getting to sea, no
matter from what port, were compelled to run the
gauntlet of the watchers in the offing. In many cases
American ships of war had been blockaded for so long
that they were hauled up shallow rivers and disman-

tled, their guns being placed in land batteries for protection from attack. Upon one occasion the English fleet had blockaded, in the harbor of New London, all the armed vessels of any consequence belonging to the Americans on the New England coast, with the exception of two.

Commodore Perry was ostensibly in command of what was known as a naval station, but he had nothing more formidable to fall back upon for active operations than a few of the old and utterly useless gunboats that had been built during the administration of Mr. Jefferson—little one-gun sloops, scarcely larger than fishing smacks.

Of course, the inactivity chafed and galled Perry's eager spirit. His trip to Washington had brought him some promise and he hoped soon to have a sea-going command. In the meantime there was nothing to do but wait.

On the evening of the 30th a seaman hurried up to Perry's house, bearing a message that a fisherman had told him that an English sloop of war had just chased a little Swedish brig on to the rocks in the harbor entrance, and that the boats of the man-o'-war had put off, evidently intending to destroy her. Immediately Perry jumped to his feet. A runner was sent into the village to call together the local company of militia, and then Perry, heading a body of sailors, made for the shore, dragging after them the only available gun, an old six-pounder.

They managed that day to fight off the boats of the sloop, but the next morning she came closer in, and under the heavy fire of her guns succeeded in landing a party who set fire to her prey. Then, having accomplished her object, she squared her yards, and taking advantage of the land breeze, put off to the southwest. Before she had gone very far, however, the sailors, under Perry's directions, had clambered down the rocks and, launching a small boat, had made their way out to the burning vessel. Without much difficulty they succeeded in putting out the flames and saved almost her entire cargo.

What had caused the English vessel to leave so hastily was soon evident, for two large barges, mounting twelve-pounders, appeared round the point. They were manned by militia companies from farther up the river that Perry had sent for the preceding evening.

All this little skirmishing must have seemed mighty small and unimportant to a man who had commanded a fleet and humbled the veterans of Nelson, but he had taken hold of the situation with all of the old thoroughness and understanding; and soon there was to come a better opportunity for the display of his gifts of leadership.

CHAPTER XI.

ALL through the months of June and July Perry was busy hastening from one place to another, in order to direct the defenses made at various points against the depredations of the British. At the little port of Wiscasset, Me., on June 26th, he repelled an attack made in considerable force by the boats of a small squadron of the enemy. Perry had all the faculties that mark leaders of men—a quick judgment of character, a firmness of purpose, a superb self-reliance, and a capacity for organization. It was this last that made him so useful to the long-shore people. Accompanied by a handful of sailors, he would appear at a threatened point, and out of the half-frightened and badly armed villagers construct a little army—skirmishers, infantry and artillery, sappers, miners, and commissary. His word of command was obeyed instantly, and his plans were followed to the letter. Besides all this, he had the wonderful personal magnetism that made men anxious to serve him. Had he been present at Wareham, Mass., on the 21st of June, the inhabitants would not have stood idly by on the

114

hills and watched the torch threaten their defenseless homes. But perhaps they were not altogether to blame, and, at the risk of digression, it might be best to tell here of the little incident that is well-nigh forgotten now, but still lingers in the traditions of eastern Massachusetts.

Early on the morning of the 21st of June, 1814, as we have stated, two or three strange sail were seen through the light fog crawling up the coast, and even before all the inhabitants could be called together by the ringing of the meeting-house bell, the hoarse bawlings of the boatswains could be heard as the anchors were let go in the little harbor. There were no cannon in the town, with the exception of an old Revolutionary six-pounder mounted near the wharf, and for that there was little powder. But still the young men and boys gathered in sufficient force to have made able resistance to a landing party. Unfortunately, however, there was none to lead them, and confusion reigned everywhere. When the fog lifted, it was seen that six large barges filled with marines and armed sailors were making in toward the land. In the leading barge was an officer waving a white flag. At once some one displayed a like signal on the pier, and soon all the boats were within hailing distance. A strange conversation now took place between the officer and one of the village selectmen, who took it upon himself to speak for his fellow-townsfolk.

" What is it that you wish? " asked the selectman, as if the intentions of the armed force from the enemy's ships could be mistaken.

" To pass the time of day," replied the officer, " and incidentally to request the gracious privilege of landing a few friends of mine, and I trust that when you hear me out you will offer no serious objections."

All the time the boats were drifting farther in, and as the officer spoke he addressed a few orders to the men nearest him. There was a smile on his lips.

" What is it you have to say? " again inquired the village spokesman. (This was not the way Master-Commandant Perry would have acted altogether.)

" We understand that there are Government stores here in great quantities, and as they must be a burden to you, we desire but to relieve you of the responsibility," was the response.

It was certainly a strange sight—the Wareham men, all with arms in their hands, crowding around the selectman, and the boats so close now that one had made fast to the wharf with a boat hook, the crew nervous, but all agrin. A hurried consultation was held by the Warehamites.

There were no public stores, in the strict sense of the word, in the town at that present moment, and a determination was reached without debate.

" If you agree to respect private property, and to seize or destroy only the munitions or stores of the

Government, you may land without molestation," said the old donkey on the wharf graciously.

"Agreed!" replied the officer. "If I am not fired upon or interfered with, private property will be left alone. But, to prove the good will of your intentions, withdraw your men to the crest of yonder hill, as it might facilitate matters and prevent blunders."

There were some mutterings among the more courageous of the villagers, but apparently there was nothing else to do, and reluctantly they withdrew up the street to the hilltop.

Now, what followed may have been an error of judgment on the part of the English lieutenant; or perhaps he reckoned wrongly in thinking he could control his men; or perhaps some reckless Yankee did not observe the letter of the unsigned treaty, and fired a shot; or maybe the Englishmen, thinking of the old adage, "All's fair in love and war," first plainly played toss with the truth. At any rate, this is what happened:

Only a short distance down the shore a vessel was building on the stocks. Hardly had half of the boats' crews scrambled on the pier when a small party, headed by the garrulous officer himself, put straight for her, and before one could say "Jack Robinson" she was going up in roaring flames. There seemed no doubt in his mind that she belonged to the State, although she was only intended to war against the peaceful cod.

The storehouses near the shore were next broken into, but most of them were empty or contained only barrels of dried fish. The old six-pounder might properly have come under the head of " material of war," and it was not spared, but was plumped into the waters of the bay. Close to the shore was an old straggling building, built partly of brick and partly of wood; it was a small cotton mill. Whether or not it was fired by order of the British commander will doubtless never be known, but, suffice it, suddenly flames burst from the windows, and in a few minutes all the wooden part was roaring merrily away, endangering the neighboring houses and threatening wholesale conflagration.

The old selectman had been restraining some of the young hot bloods with difficulty. Badly armed and equipped, they would have stood little chance against the marines and sailors if they had ventured to attack them, and perhaps discretion was the better part in this case. But when the English were about to take to their boats again, down the hill stalked the old man, followed by a dozen or so of the village elders.

" Your conduct has been outrageous, sir! " thundered one of the latter, shaking his fist in the lieutenant's face.

" You have broken your sacred promise! " put in another.

" Seize these men! " said the lieutenant angrily,

in reply, and before they knew it the twelve elders were bundled over the side of the pier into the boats.

The people gathered on the hill made a rush, but the officer, who must have been a cool one, slipped a pistol from his belt and confronted them.

" If a shot is fired, it will be so much the worse for your friends! " he shouted, and then, without hurrying, he stepped down into his barge.

All this goes to show what lack of proper leadership will do. If Perry and his faithful body guard of sixteen Jack tars had been there, the story would have been different. He would not have allowed a flag of truce to be accompanied by six boat loads of armed men.

But to return to the poor captives in the stern sheets of the barges. Their protestations were of no avail, and some, who saw before them a long term of imprisonment as " English sailors," broke down completely. But when they had reached the fleet the ranking officer assured them that they had nothing to fear, and they were put ashore some four miles below the town.

Now, all this angered Perry to such an extent that in his report of the affair he asked to have more adequate means given him to prevent the recurrence of these incursions, and during the month following he was busy organizing the militia and establishing a coast guard in his district. But soon he was to leave

for very active service, although he received no orders
to take part in it, and it was his own dauntless and ad-
venturous spirit that dictated his movements.

Long weeks before this—in fact, shortly after the
battle of Erie—Perry had been promised the command
of the new frigate Java, then building at the city of
Baltimore. He had been present at the laying of her
keel, and since that day, although far from the spot,
he had kept interested in her plans and development.
She had grown to be the apple of his eye, and he was
looking forward eagerly to the day when he should
tread her quarter-deck and once more feel that he
was a sailor. His life at Newport, surrounded by family and friends, was pleasant and happy, but his nature rebelled against the inactivity.

One day there came to him the news that the
enemy had landed in great force in Virginia and Maryland, that a battle had been fought, the Americans
routed, and Washington, the capital city, had been
burned, and that the shores of the Chesapeake were
threatened. Baltimore was in danger, and perhaps
Perry's mind dwelt for a moment on the beautiful
frigate in the shipyard.

At any rate, his place was where he could serve
his country, and without hesitation he packed up a few
belongings, sailor fashion, and started top speed for
the seat of war.

All the subsequent happenings require some introduction, and it is best to make a separate chapter telling of the important doings that were then casting great gloom and trouble throughout the country; for our arms on land had suffered serious reverses, and had it not been for the brilliant actions of our little navy on the high seas, the nation would have been in a very depressed mood indeed.

CHAPTER XII.

OFF TO THE SOUTH.

BLADENSBURG, Md., is a little town but a few miles from the city of Washington. It is within easy driving distance, and in the year 1814 was nothing but a sleepy village, with a few scattering houses on the wooded slopes of the surrounding hills. It was a famous meeting place for duelists in those old days, and many "affairs of honor" were settled there; but it is chiefly known as being the battle ground of one of the most disastrous meetings between our troops and those of the invading English—disastrous to the American arms, perhaps, in its immediate consequences only, as it had small effect upon the general conduct of the war, but none the less hard to bear for all that. As it was the news of this battle that brought Perry to the scene as fast as horses could bring him over the hundreds of miles of rough roads, it is easy to see how important a place the village then took in the minds of the country at large, for it was the gate through which the British entered for the destruction of the capital of the country.

On the 24th of August the little army that had

landed from the Chesapeake fleet marched on Washington, under the command of the British general
Ross. The total force was not far from five thousand men, consisting of regulars, marines, and sailors
equipped as infantry. But horsemen were out all
through the countryside, calling the militia to rally,
and warning the inhabitants of the enemy's approach.
They gathered at Bladensburg from all directions, and
at noon everything was in great confusion. There
seemed to be no head of affairs among the motley collection of farmers, armed with everything from rifles
to brass blunderbusses. A small detachment of American regulars, numbering some three hundred and fifty,
and a few volunteers from the Potomac River and
the city of Washington, under the command of Commodore Joshua Barney, composed the backbone of
the American body, and did most of the resistance.

The battle opened at one o'clock, and it was soon
perceived that the lack of training and discipline of the
raw militia, and the dearth of proper leadership, fore-
told defeat, although the enemy were tired by a long
march and fatigued by the heat of the day, for it was
scorching hot. There is not time or space to describe
the action here, but the militia did not stand well
under fire, and seemed to lack all principle of organ-
ized fighting. But there was much to be said in their
defense. The majority were old men and boys, and
a great proportion did not arrive until after the battle

had begun. Commodore Barney and his little band stood firm, as did the regulars, and the loss of killed and wounded was among them mostly, the brave old sailor being wounded and taken prisoner late in the afternoon. Before sunset the vanguard of the English had entered Washington.

English historians make no excuse for the doings that followed, and General Ross and some of his officers quite congratulated themselves on what was probably as great a piece of vandalism as was ever perpetrated in "civilized warfare," for the torch was applied to the Capitol, the President's house, and to all the public buildings; even some private edifices suffered, and all of the important records and documents were destroyed in the library.

The navy yard had been set on fire by order of the American officer in command, to prevent important munitions of war from falling into the hands of the invaders. On the following evening the English left Washington in haste, for the forces of the surrounding country were gathering, and so sudden was their departure that they left behind almost all of their wounded for the Americans to take care of. In the meantime a portion of their naval force had proceeded up the river as far as Alexandria, on the Virginia shore. The town was absolutely without defenses, as the only fort that could serve as any protection had been abandoned and destroyed.

This was the state of affairs that Perry found ex-
isting when he arrived at Washington—a terror-
stricken community, and stark and blackened ruins of
what had been the finest buildings in the country.
But he was glad to find some of his old comrades of
the Tripolitan war gathered there for the same purpose as his own—namely, to offer their services in any
capacity for the further protection of the State or for
the punishment of the enemy. Among them were
Rogers and Porter, both of whom had gained honor
and distinction on the high seas in command of Yankee ships, and now they were eager to serve on land
and turn soldier for the time being, without much
chance for glory.

The poor inhabitants of Alexandria had been
forced to take the English practically to their homes
and hearthstones, for, in addition to delivering up all
public property in the town, they were compelled to
feed the fleet and to work night and day at raising
some small craft that had been sunk in the river. The
English commander paid for all this, it must be con-
fessed, but the payment was made in bills on the English Government, which were somewhat difficult of
collection, it can be easily perceived, and were valuable as autographs and mementoes, hardly more.

Rogers and Porter and Perry found plenty to do,
and but little time in which to do it. There were
forces to organize, batteries to build, and expeditions

to drive the enemy out of the position he then held in the river. One of them—an attempt to surprise and dislodge the British ships by means of a small flotilla of fire vessels—failed because of lack of wind; and when, on the 6th of September, the enemy moved down the river, the hastily constructed batteries were not heavy enough to successfully oppose or cope with the English guns.

Perry had taken command of one of the hurriedly improvised forts that had been erected on the shore at a place known as Indian Head (now the Government proving ground for heavy ordnance). He knew that the few six-pounder cannon he had would prove most ineffectual, and he lent all his efforts to secure and mount some guns of larger caliber; but most of them had been destroyed in the navy yard, and the case looked hopeless. At last he was informed that some miles away there was an old eighteen-pound gun, a relic of the Revolution. Whether or not there was time to place it in position was doubtful, but he determined to try, and so close did he " make connections," that he had mounted the gun but a few minutes before the firing up the river told him of the approach of the fleet.

As he supposed, the fire of the six-pounders amounted to nothing ; but that one heavy piece, aimed and fired by the " hero of Erie " himself, delayed the enemy for over an hour, and directed against that single gun were the broadsides of two frigates, two sloops, and five smaller gunboats.

How long this spunky little battery would have annoyed the British vessels is mere guesswork, but the powder ran out, and then, and not till then, did Perry order his men to retire. When he came to reckon up his losses, he found to his delight that he had lost no men and had but one slightly wounded.

But the enemy had disappeared down the river, and a consultation of officers was held in Washington to determine what would be the best plan to follow in order to harass them and prevent a recurrence of such things as had taken place at the capital.

Perry and Commodore Rogers were sure that the next point of attack would be the city of Baltimore, and, leaving the ruined town, they repaired thither posthaste. How right they were in their surmise will be told in another chapter.

CHAPTER XIII.

COMMODORE PERRY sat in the coffee room of the Fountain Inn at Baltimore. He had pulled off his boots, that were plashed and muddy, and was lying back in an easy-chair, gazing out of the window. It seemed hard to imagine that only a short time before, in the big dining room at this same tavern, he had been given a dinner and reception the like of which had never been equaled in the country up to that time. Now, here he was at the same place, but the conditions of his visit were entirely different. He had come thither as a volunteer to fight in the defense of the city whose citizens had extended him such open-handed hospitality.

The enemy were at their very doors. The large fleet in the Chesapeake, acting under orders of the British admirals Cochrane and Cockburn, had been concentrated for an attack on Fort McHenry and the batteries of Covington and the Lazaretto. Only the day previous a little battle had been fought near Moorsfields between a detachment of English sailors and marines that had formed a landing party from one

of the frigates and three companies of Maryland volunteers under Colonel Read. Although no details of
the action were then known in the city, the fact that
the British had retreated to their vessels had occasioned much rejoicing.

It was only the day before that Perry had paid a
visit to the vessel that was to be his future command,
the Java. She was almost finished, and he had looked
with pride at the great fabric as she lay there at anchor
off the shipyard. It would be a bitter personal disap-
pointment to him if he should have to lose her, but
he knew well enough that nothing would so delight
the hearts of the English leaders as to set fire to her.
But Perry also well knew that the volunteers and
militia of Pennsylvania and Maryland that had gathered for the protection of the city were of a different
caliber from the ill-disciplined and poorly equipped
countrymen that had met the enemy at Bladensburg.

Hearing the door of the coffee room open suddenly,
Perry rose and turned in time to meet a rain-soaked
figure in a greatcoat, whose voluminous folds wrapped
him from head to foot. The stranger threw off the
heavy cloak and stamped his feet hard upon the floor,
sending the mud flying in all directions.

"Well met, indeed, commodore!" exclaimed Perry,
as he recognized in the dim light the weather-beaten
features of Commodore Rogers.

"I have news for you, sir," said the latter, speaking in his gruff but cordial voice, " and news that may perhaps surprise you."

" Out with it, then," Perry exclaimed, " for I'm all impatience. Have you heard from the fight of yesterday? "

" 'Tis just that that I wish to speak with you about," Rogers returned. " I have seen Read, and interviewed some of his prisoners. Sir Peter Parker, who was in command of the Menelaus, was killed in the fight—shot by one of Read's riflemen. His body was taken on board the ship, and she has now dropped down the bay to join the rest of the squadron. How I should like to measure yardarms with her in the old Constitution! "

Perry did not reply for a minute. He remembered having seen the Menelaus before the outbreak of the war, and upon one occasion he had met Sir Peter, when he was a young lieutenant in the Mediterranean.

" One could not wish for a braver or more gallant opponent," he said. " I should much have liked the honor of meeting him myself. But we have turned soldiers now, commodore, or, better, you have turned artilleryman. I am anything they may choose to make of me."

" True enough what you say of me," Rogers returned; " and to-morrow, if the enemy attack us, I shall have charge of the flotilla men of the city batteries. I have some good old men-o'-war's men under

me—truculent fellows, who will answer for their guns,
I warrant you. What post will you take, sir?"

"I have been busy helping Webster at Fort Covington, and expect to hear to-night to what position
I shall be assigned," Perry rejoined. "Unless I am
wrong and miss my reckoning altogether, to-morrow
will prove an eventful day for all of us."

"I well believe that," Rogers replied, "but I re-
joice to say that we are prepared, and that General
Stricker has under him three of the best regiments in
the regular service. There is nothing like a touch of
the disciplined and professional fighting man to steady
the nerves of the volunteer."

"Yes, methinks that our friend General Ross may
meet with a surprise on the morrow." Perry said this
with a half smile, for since the affair at Washington
Ross's boasting had reached the ears of the Americans.

Rogers had stepped to the door, and was roaring
down the hall lustily for the "Boots" to come and
take his muddy foot gear, and when this was accomplished he turned to Perry again.

"Ross says that he will take the city, and he doesn't
care if it rains militia. It's more likely to rain lead and
iron, and I trust it will be to his liking. But there is
more news," the old sailor added, hitching up his chair
closer to Perry's. "We have discovered the whole plan
of the English force now in our waters."

"And how did that come about, pray, may I

ask?" questioned Perry, straightening up and listening eagerly.

"A letter was found in the pocket of a young English officer dead in the field, and, if it is true that his information was correct, we can see how important they regard the capture of this city in making up their schedule. I saw the letter myself, and I can tell you that it was most interesting reading. But knowledge of an enemy's intentions is much like getting the weather gauge of him—an advantage that, by the way, we know all about, commodore, eh?"

"But the plan?" interposed Perry. "Have they any definite object in hovering along the coast?"

"That they have, indeed," Rogers answered, "and in substance it is as follows: From this letter it would seem that the plan was not left to the admirals, but was devised at nothing less than a cabinet meeting previous to the departure of the fleets from England. It was the intention to capture and destroy the city of Washington—in which, alas! they have unfortunately been so successful; then to follow with the attack and destruction of this city, Charleston, and Savannah, and to end up the whole matter with a concentration of forces upon New Orleans. It is for this latter purpose that the great fleet is gathering at the Bermudas. Ship after ship is coming in there loaded down with the victors of the Peninsula; and, moreover, they are intending to make out of the southern portion of Louisiana a British dependency. There is assurance for you!"

"It strikes me," observed Perry, looking out the window at the rainy street, " that they are taking much for granted. 'In stormy latitudes never reckon on a fair wind until you get it,' is a good motto."

"I seem to feel it in my bones that we will be successful to-morrow," observed the older man, " and God grant that this part of their programme and all that is to follow will go sadly astray!"

"Amen to that!" said Perry. "I think they would give a good deal to lay their hands upon the new frigate building at the yards."

"Indeed they would," Rogers answered, " and that would disappoint some one I know most terribly."

Although it was not publicly announced that Perry was to have command of the Java, it was well known in the service that he had been promised her, and few there were who begrudged him the honor; for, although the separate victories at sea had added glory and luster to the little American navy, Perry's was the only one that might really be said to be of national importance. This was universally recognized, and historians of the later day have not failed to dwell upon the fact.

But to return to the two old comrades and their conversation.

"Her very name," said Commodore Rogers, referring to the last subject spoken of, "is a thorn in the flesh of every English officer. I should like to take her into the English Channel, or, better, anchor her under the guns of Gibraltar or Malta."

"So should I," Perry returned, mentally adding to himself the words, "And some day I mean to."

At this moment the tap boy appeared with candles, for it was growing dark, and set about preparing a table in the corner of the room. Soon both officers were seated.

"It is too bad that Porter is not here to enjoy this," Rogers observed, washing down a mouthful of mutton pasty with a swallow of port wine.

"It is, indeed," Perry returned. "And now I'll propose a toast: Here's to success of our arms on land and sea; here's to officers and men. Here's to straight shots, brave hearts, and to each star on our flag!"

"And lasting confusion to the enemies of America," added Commodore Rogers.

Then both rose to their feet and drank the toast standing. Hardly had they finished their meal and settled themselves down in the easy-chairs again when a wet and bedraggled messenger, in a uniform that proclaimed him to be half soldier and half sailor, appeared at the door.

"General Stricker's compliments, gentlemen," he said. "All officers are ordered to report to their posts."

"I suppose that means us," Rogers observed, rising hastily. "No sleep in a bed for me this night."

"Nor for me either," returned Perry, following the elder officer to the door, where Rogers was roaring once more for his boots and greatcoat.

A few minutes later they had both passed out into the dark, rainy night. All through the city messengers were hurrying, and a body of troops, following the tap of a rain-soaked drum, swept by the corner on the double-quick.

CHAPTER XIV.

DEFENDING THE CITY.

WHEN day broke after the storm there was a strange sight to be seen. Off the mouth of the Patapsco River lay huddled a fleet of forty-two sail. Taking advantage of the light wind and favorable tide, they had crept close in to land late the previous evening, with boats out carefully feeling their way ahead of them with a lead.

The heaviest ships of the line had been anchored across the channel, while the sloops of war and smaller craft, that had been lightened to decrease their draught, worked their way nearer to shore.

It was an anxious moment for the American forces in the trenches and small forts that had been erected for the defense of the city. The landing place that the British had chosen was some twelve miles distant, and, unfortunately, at that point no batteries had been erected to oppose them. Late in the afternoon some five thousand redcoats and four thousand marines had reached the shore in safety, and by the morning of the 12th they were in readiness to begin their advance.

136

In the meantime the frigates had made their way up the river, and with sixteen bomb vessels had anchored within about two miles of Fort McHenry.

And now, although the hero of Erie bore no prominent part in the operations that followed, it is well to describe the condition of affairs and all that passed under his immediate observation.

Fort McHenry was commanded by Lieutenant-Colonel George Armistead, of the United States artillery; at the Lazaretto was stationed Lieutenant Rutter, at the head of some artillerymen, sailors, and volunteers; and at Fort Covington were Rogers and Lieutenant Newcomb, of the navy, with a force of about three hundred men. Near by was a six-gun battery that had been hastily erected and placed under command of Lieutenant Webster. Back of this were lines of intrenchments and breastworks, behind which lay hidden the militia and the volunteers from the city of Baltimore, who had bravely turned out almost to a man.

In all, at the forts and batteries there were about twelve hundred men, while the inner lines of fortifications sheltered perhaps four thousand. All the forces were under the command of Major-General Samuel Smith, who was assisted by General Winder, of the United States army, and by General Stricker, of Baltimore. Stricker's brigade, composed principally of riflemen and infantry and Pennsylvania and Maryland

10

volunteers, had been dispatched to intercept the advance of the British invasion, that was headed by General Ross, seconded by none less than Admiral Cochrane himself, who commanded the marine detachment.

This was the position at ten o'clock on the morning of the 12th. Scouts had brought back the news of the enemy's approach, and by two o'clock in the afternoon shots were exchanged between the outposts of General Stricker's brigade and the enemy, who had pushed on four miles thus far without meeting any opposition.

Beyond all doubt General Ross was congratulating himself upon the ease with which he was going to duplicate the taking of Washington.

The American artillery opened fire with great fierceness upon the British front, and the action became general, the Fifth and Twenty-seventh regulars sustaining the brunt of the attack in a splendid manner. But the American forces were greatly outnumbered, and, owing to the length of the enemy's lines and the situation of the ground, Stricker found it impossible after a while to use artillery or cavalry to any advantage, and thus the main defense was made by the muskets of the foot soldiers and the rifles of a small detachment of sharpshooters posted on the left of the line. So rapid and effective was the fire that this small body of perhaps seventeen hundred men succeeded in stopping the enemy's forward movement;

and it was here that General Ross met his doom, falling with several other British officers as he emerged
at the head of his column from a small patch of
woods.

Now, owing to the fact that Stricker feared that
his flank might be turned, and that if this happened
he would be cut off from re-enforcements, he retreated
slowly, back upon the line of intrenchments before the
city.

The American loss was trifling compared with
that of the English; and Colonel Brooke, who had succeeded to the command at the death of General Ross,
advanced no farther than the line which General
Stricker had held, and there encamped.

It was a busy night for the Americans. There was
no rest for them. Picks and shovels were plied indus-
triously, and when the next day dawned all the intrenchments had been strengthened, and new earthworks had been thrown up completely covering the
lines of attack. Not much was accomplished this day
by either side, although Colonel Brooke pushed forward to within a mile of the trenches, drove in some
of the outposts, and by nightfall was apparently preparing for an attack in the darkness. But nothing
occurred to break the stillness, although Stricker's
force slept upon their arms, prepared for instant action.

General Stricker, who had gone down to the front
with some men of Stansbury's and Foreman's brigade,

which was entirely made up of seamen and marines taken from the command under Commodore Rogers, looked out over the breastworks at dawn of the 14th. He had walked to the front in company with Captain Bird, who was then in command of the United States dragoons, and from the vantage point which they had selected he could look down the road toward the position of the enemy's encampment.

It had been a pitch-dark night, and the rain had fallen heavily. The roads were muddy, and the earthworks had been almost washed away in some places; the trenches where the American troops had passed the night were ankle-deep in water. The poor men were tired, and for three days had been soaked to the skin; yet they were all prepared for the battle which no one doubted would take place, for the guns of the fleet had been pounding all the night at the forts on the water front.

As the general looked toward the woods, and as the light broadened, he turned to Captain Bird, who was at his elbow.

"Surely, I think, captain," he said, "that if the enemy were there we would see something of him by this time, and I judge that we would have heard from him also. Do you think it possible that he could have left?"

"I hardly think so," was the captain's rejoinder. "It was reported that they were waiting for re-enforcements, but no outposts being visible does seem strange, I'll grant you."

Evidently the stillness and lack of movement at the front had attracted the attention of other officers also, and the curiosity of the men themselves had been aroused, for all along the line heads appeared, and soon the earthworks were black with watching figures. Presently a half score of men, under orders of General Stricker, darted out across the fields toward where the British had been, some following the road and others boldly plunging into the woods. Not a sound was heard, and soon some of the men were seen returning on the run.

The enemy had retreated! Soon the bugles were singing for the cavalry and the dragoons to start in pursuit. Perhaps the English had discovered that it had "rained militia" with a vengeance.

So much for the doings on the land side of the city approaches, and now let us return to the operations of the English fleet that on the 12th we had left anchored in the form of a semicircle in front of the forts and the city batteries, but outside of gunshot.

It was here that one of the most stirring scenes of the war had been enacted, and one that had been immediately under Perry's eyes and in which he had taken no small part. Fort McHenry was about two miles below the city, and on the morning of the 13th six bomb vessels and several armed with the destructive rockets that the English then employed had begun an attack that had been continued unceasingly until three o'clock in the afternoon; but owing to the distance chosen by the English commander, little harm had been done up to that hour, and the Americans had reserved their fire until the vessels should approach within the range at which their ordnance could accomplish some results. This may have encouraged the Englishmen in their attack, but the fierce fire that they received was now too much for them. From the fort and shore batteries shot and shell rained down upon them, and but a few minutes was enough to compel them to slip their cables and wear off.

Great was the satisfaction and delight of the Americans, who thought they saw in this evidences that the enemy wished to discontinue the struggle; but all those of greater experience knew that such a slight discomfiture could produce no lasting result, and that the bulldog courage and tenacity of the English would lead them to much further and more active demonstrations.

While the forces under General Stricker were busily engaged in the night throwing up earthworks, the artillerymen and the "sea-fencibles," as the sailors were called, were eagerly on the lookout, and the crews slept about their guns, seeking shelter in the

bastions and under the improvised tents in the pouring and continuous rain.

At ten o'clock Rogers and Perry, who were sleep-
ing in a little house near the Covington fort, were
aroused by a knocking on the door, and they were
ready in an instant for any action.

An old quartermaster who was acting as a sergeant of artillery stood there with his tarpaulin hat
in his hand, the rain trickling down his grizzled
face.

" There seems to be some movement out in the
river," he said. " At least, one of the sentries reported
that he heard the click of a capstan, and that some
of the vessels are getting at their anchor."

" A night attack, perhaps," observed Perry.

" I expected as much," returned Rogers; " but
we have better guns this time than we had last
week on the Potomac, and we'll make it warm for
them."

When they reached the shore all listened intently,
but nothing could be heard. All at once Perry grasped
Rogers by the arm.

" Oars! Do you hear them? Yes, plainly, off there
to the right. Listen! "

" Oars, sure enough," Rogers returned, and, calling the quartermaster, he turned out the guard and
passed the word that the enemy were ascending the
Patapsco.

Word was sent to the Lazaretto and the city batteries, and also to inform the barges that were anchored close inshore, off the wharves.

While the American troops were hastening to their stations and everything was being made ready to prepare for an attack, which they supposed would take place at daylight, a cheer was heard from up the river, and bright gashes of flame ripped out against the darkness.

It was then perceived that a number of English barges with muffled oars had passed by the batteries and entered the river, in order to attack the forts and the city from the rear. Even the cheering of the Englishmen out in the water could be heard distinctly, and, as if at a signal, their first gun had been answered by tremendous cannonading from the great vessels that were anchored in line opposite the fort. The glare of their guns lit the heavens, and the fiery paths of their rockets as they shot in toward the forts seamed and crossed the cloudy night.

All along the shore the American batteries replied, their fire being principally directed against the barges, whose position was outlined by the flash of their own firing. The scene was magnificent and sublime, and one American, then present as a prisoner on board one of the English vessels, was so inspired by the sight that he has described it in verses that will last

through the ages—as long as America has Americans
to sing her praises, and a flag that represents liberty,
courage, and humanity.

The Star-spangled Banner then sprang into life
from the pen of Francis Scott Key, and all the school
children who have sung it, and all those who know it
by heart, have a complete picture in verse of the bombardment of Fort McHenry.

It would seem that the long bombardment of the
13th and the terrific cannonading of the night following would have almost smothered the little fort, but
what does the poet say?

"O say, can you see by the dawn's early light
    What so proudly we hailed at the twilight's last gleaming,
Whose broad stripes and bright stars, through the perilous fight,
    O'er the ramparts we watched were so gallantly streaming?
And the rockets' red glare, the bombs bursting in air,
Gave proof through the night that our flag was still there.
Oh! say, does that star-spangled banner yet wave
O'er the land of the free and the home of the brave?

"On the shore, dimly seen through the mists of the deep,
    Where the foe's haughty host in dread silence reposes,
What is that which the breeze, o'er the towering steep,
    As it fitfully blows, half conceals, half discloses?
Now it catches the gleam of the morning's first beam,
In full glory reflected now shines on the stream.
'Tis the star-spangled banner! Oh, long may it wave
O'er the land of the free and the home of the brave!"

What a joy it must have been to the eyes of all the Americans to have seen that flag floating over the ramparts when day broke!

Occasionally Major Armistead would reply with a gun, in order to let those farther up the river know that he was yet in the land of the living.

The fleet was not damaged to any extent, but with the venturesome barges it was another story. Rogers's crew at Fort Covington and all the flotilla men poured into them such a destructive fire that only the darkness and their ceasing to reply saved them from complete annihilation. Two of the barges were sunk, and in the rest that managed to escape were many dead and wounded. The loss sustained by the Americans on shore was trifling in comparison.

By seven o'clock on the morning of the 14th the British fire ceased. The vessels drew off into the Chesapeake, and Baltimore was saved.

A contemporary writer makes a comment on the action in one of the "morals" that writers of that day apparently attempted to draw from almost every occurrence, but it is so apt in this connection that it might be well to quote it:

"The disastrous result of this attack on Baltimore by a formidable land and naval force flushed with victory and confident of success adds another to the many evidences which the history of human affairs has furnished, that it does not belong to man to boast of his strength or achievements, and much less to indulge in sentiments of contempt for others." All of which is very true.

As soon as it was seen that Baltimore was no longer to be the object of attack, Commodore Perry's duties at his own station called him to the North, and he set out with all speed for Newport.

CHAPTER XV.

A RESCUE.

The early winter of 1816 passed by uneventfully, except for one exciting experience that will be related hereafter in this chapter.

Perry was but thirty-one years of age, and yet at this time he was perhaps Newport's most distinguished and important citizen. If anything happened where action and direction were needed in the superintendence of the men at work, Perry was called upon. His appearance at a fire, for instance, was a signal for all to report to him for orders; and so used had he become to thus always holding himself in readiness for any emergency that it was said that he "slept with his boots on."

During the year 1815 he had been busily engaged in getting the Java ready to proceed to sea. She now lay in the harbor of Newport, under Perry's eye, and not a stick had been put into her that he had not inspected, and he knew the quality of every foot of the standing rigging and running gear. He was hoping that as soon as the inclement weather was over he should be sent to the Mediterranean,

but time sped on, and he stayed quietly at Newport.

On the 10th of January, 1816, while he was seated
in his study reading, there came a knock on the door,
and a breathless sailor stood there twirling his hat in
his hands.

"Well, my man, what can I do for you?" Perry
inquired, in the rather fatherly tone that marks the
officer when addressing a man of his own crew.

"A messenger's arrived from Brenton's Neck, sir,"
spoke up the man, "with the information that a vessel is stranded on the reefs there, sir, and they say
that there are several men to be seen lashed to the
rigging. God help them in such weather as this!"

It was blowing very hard. The dry, powdery snow
swept over the ground into little drifts under the lee
of every tree and fence-post. The waters of the bay
looked black and angry, tossed and crossed by a succession of feathery white caps. If one listened, the
booming of the heavy surf against the icy rocks beyond the harbor could be heard from the southward.

"Step inside, my man," said Perry, ushering the
sailor into the spacious hallway. "I will immediately
repair to the yard. But, hold! perhaps it is better
for me to prepare them for my coming. You will
hurry there ahead of me, and tell the bargemen to
meet me at the fish basin and have the barge ready
to be put into the water."

"Ay, ay, sir!" the man returned, touching his cap. "I'm not a bargeman myself, but a right good oar, sir; ten years a whaler and four years in the Constitution. If there's a vacancy in the boat, might I ask for it?"

"It is yours," Perry replied. "Report ready for duty."

In fifteen minutes the commodore was seen coming down the snow-covered walk. The group of men huddled in the lee of the Government building stepped out to meet him and drew up at attention.

The coxswain of the barge saluted. "I've been down to see the wreck, sir," he said. "She is in plain sight from the rocks on the other side, but I doubt her holding together long. She's pounding very bad, sir."

"Are the men still on her?" asked Perry quickly.

"Yes, sir ; I could count eleven in the mizzen rigging."

Perry glanced at the crew. Inside in the sheltered waters of the bay it was rough and tumbling. What must it be outside, where the broad sweep of the Atlantic dashed in toward the iron-bound coast? The air was full of tiny icy particles, that stung the face and eyes and matted the hair and eyebrows; but, headed by the commodore, the men marched down to the basin, where the big barge swung from davits under the shelter of a roof shed that extended over the water.

It was the work but of a minute to lower her away, and Perry noticed with satisfaction that there was a place in the thwarts for the ex-whaleman who had been so anxious to accompany him. There were no laggards in the crew, but some of the men shook their heads ominously as they looked out toward the mouth of the harbor.

"Come, my lads," cried Perry cheerily as he stepped into the stern sheets, "we are going to the rescue and relief of shipwrecked seamen!"

In another instant he had given the order to shove off, and the men were bending at their oars.

As they got out beyond the end of Goat Island the full force of the wind was felt. It seemed as if the barge at first made little headway even under the impetus of the twelve pairs of sturdy arms. The short, choppy seas thumped under the broad bow, and shot up constant jets of icy water that deluged the men from head to foot. But it was seen that they were gaining, and slowly the barge crept out to the harbor mouth, and there they began to feel the heave of the great surges that rolled in from the southward.

The strong set of the tide at one time threatened to bring them in dangerously near to the point, but by strenuous efforts they weathered it, and, once clear of the land, the wreck of the schooner could be seen jammed on the reef not far from where the lightship now swings its warning.

"Now, my lads," cried Perry, "there she is! Get your backs into your work. Pull all together!"

The seamen, with set teeth, were putting every ounce they possessed into the backward heave, but the wind was blowing with terrific force. It threatened, as they lifted their oars out of the water, to tear them out of their hands. The barge would hang for a minute on the top of a wave, and then go racing down into a hollow so deep that those watching on shore would hold their breath. But inch by inch she gained against the wind.

The cold and benumbed seamen on the schooner gave a feeble cheer as they saw what a fight was being made to reach them. Over an hour it took to row that scant two miles—an hour of constant heartbreaking work that none but the hardiest constitutions could have survived.

The whaleman was pulling port stroke, and every now and then he would forget the man-o'-war training and call out the old whaling phrases of encouragement:

"Now for ten good strokes, and ten more on top of 'em! Pull as if you was to win a wife, lads! Lift the sides out of her now!" and so on.

The men would double their efforts, and soon but a half cable's length separated them from the shuddering, tottering wreck. The white-topped seas were breaking completely over her. Her bow was gone clear from the fore chains, and but little of her quarter-deck was above the water.

Perry saw as he stood up, steadying himself with one hand on the coxswain's shoulder, that the wreck could hold together but a few minutes longer.

It requires great skill to approach a stranded vessel in a heavy seaway, where there is danger, even when one is to leeward, that a back set may grind the rescuing boat to pieces against the sides of the wreck; but, after one unsuccessful attempt, Perry managed to get a rope passed between the barge and what was left of the schooner, and to his delight he counted eleven men still alive on board of her, although some were almost incapable of movement, and but for the strong lashings that bound them to the rigging would have been swept off long before.

Few of the men had strength enough to help the barge's crew work in closer, but with great skill all were taken in over the bow and passed aft to the stern sheets. It was fortunate, indeed, that she was so large and able a sea boat, and could hold them all in comfort and safety. The men were busy fending off pieces of wreckage that threatened to stave in the barge's sides, and it was a great relief when they cast off the bow line and turned the head in toward the shore.

11

It was very different now, coming down before the wind. They would sway upon the top of a shouldering sea, tear along with its seething crest, and then apparently wait for another to heave them in toward the harbor mouth. Before they reached it the wrecked craft went all to pieces. In ten minutes they were almost under the shelter of the neck, and in less than half an hour the barge and her happy crew were safely in the basin, where a large crowd had gathered to greet the rescuers and the rescued. The cheers of the Java's men sounded above the gale.

The wrecked vessel proved to be the schooner Eliza, commanded and owned by Captain Charles Gorton, a Newport man. Most of the crew were Rhode Islanders also, and Perry's popularity in the State grew into a deep affection, that was felt for him by all the inhabitants thereof.

A contemporary writer, in referring to this rescue, and after describing the manner of it, wrote as follows:

" This simple occurrence speaks more forcibly than the most elaborate panegyric in proof of the humane and benevolent heart of Perry. We here behold the same man who upon Lake Erie, clothed with all the terrors of war, was himself a host to the enemy, engaging in spirit and alacrity in an enterprise not to meet and conquer the enemy; not to acquire glory and renown, and swell the expansive note of his own fame; not to defend the rights of his country, but to aid suffering humanity, or, to use his own appropriate words, ' to relieve shipwrecked seamen.' "

But Perry dismissed the whole subject from his mind, and, like the simple and grave character that he was, regarded it merely as an incident.

Weeks went by, and he grew more and more impatient for the sailing orders to come that would dispatch him and his fine vessel to European waters. The crew were the pick of the service, and the vessel, he knew, was second to none of her class in all the world.

CHAPTER XVI.

DURING the early months of 1815-'16 the American flag was shown in the Mediterranean flying from the masts of the largest and most powerful fleets that the new country had ever sent out. Decatur, in April of the year 1815, had sailed from New York with a squadron consisting of the Guerrière, Constellation, and Macedonian, frigates; the Ontario and Epervier, sloops of war; and the schooners Flambeau, Spark, Spitfire, and Torch. Shortly afterward this squadron was followed by another under Commodore Bainbridge, who upon his arrival superseded Decatur in supreme command.

There was a reason for all this display of force, for the Barbary states of Tunis and Algiers had once more given evidence of evil intentions. Probably they thought that, after having had a war with so powerful a nation as Great Britain, the United States would have no war vessels left to defend her merchant ships, and probably their turbaned high mightinesses concluded that the chance was too good to be missed. At any rate, they both started upon the rampage, and

COMMODORE OLIVER HAZARD PERRY, U. S. N.

(From Freeman's engraving of the painting by J. W. Jarvis.)

were more than mightily surprised when the American squadron, headed by the seventy-four Independence, arrived off their respective capitals and threatened punishment; and they came down from their attitude in short order, after having had one or two little actions, and from that day forward the United States paid no tribute to the Algerian pirates, and a citizen of that country was as safe in Tunis or Tripoli or Algiers as he would be upon the streets of Philadelphia.

So much for the influence of sea power properly displayed.

The Dey of Algiers was said to have remarked to the British consul at that port:

"You told us that the American navy would be destroyed in six months by you, and now they make war upon us with two of your own vessels that they have taken from you."

What the British officer replied to this is not on record.

Perry had longed to accompany these expeditions, and it was to enforce the effect that they had made that Commodore Chauncey was dispatched, in March, 1816, to the same waters. The Java sailed out later and joined the squadron at Port Mahon. She carried with her the ratified treaty that had been drawn up between Algiers and this country.

Again the dey attempted to cut up rough, and

denied that he had sanctioned the treaty (his own seal and signature were there appended); but when Chauncey sailed into the harbor he changed his mind again, and concluded that it was best for him to stop his foolishness.

And now we come to a chapter in the life of Commodore Perry that deals with an entirely personal side of his history and character, and is yet of such interest that the public has a claim on it.

It happened, alas! that on board the Java at this time there was a Captain John Heath, who commanded the marines on the vessel. What sort of a man he was we can only judge by his actions. It is true he found some supporters for his methods and doings, but we have only to take from the records of the investigation and court-martial that followed the facts to be related, and these are simply that Commodore Perry, provoked and incensed by what he considered insulting conduct of an inferior officer, raised his hand against a man dressed in the uniform of an officer in the service of the nation.

With great frankness and directness he himself related the incident in a letter to Commodore Chauncey, then commanding the squadron. As it gives a history of the quarrel and explains Perry's position, at the same time giving further insight into his character, we publish it here just as it came from his pen:

"UNITED STATES SHIP JAVA, TUNIS BAY, *October 8, 1816.*

"SIR: I am under the painful necessity of informing you of a circumstance and of detailing to you the causes which led to an event of a very unpleasant nature.

"The apparent violation of the laws of my country which may be imputed to me, in having offered personal violence to the captain of the marine guard of this ship, I trust will be in a great measure extenuated by the consideration that, although I do not absolutely defend this mode of redress, yet I insist the consequences were produced by a sufficient provocation.

"The general deportment of Captain Heath toward me, so contrary to the usual address of my officers, and, moreover, his marked insolence to me in many instances, induced me to believe that his conduct proceeded from a premeditated determination to insult me on every occasion.

"His palpable neglect of duty on several important emergencies, together with the usual indolence and inattention to the calls of his office, made it a desirable object with me to solicit his removal the first convenient opportunity, not only to obtain a more active and vigilant officer, but to save him the rigorous severity of a court-martial.

"I now, sir, narrate to you the circumstances which have thus compelled me to address you.

"On the evening of the 16th of September last, while this ship lay at anchor in the harbor of Messina, two of her marines deserted by jumping overboard and swimming on shore. Informed of the fact, Captain Heath, as their commanding officer, was immediately sent for and acquainted therewith; but he refused to go on deck, alleging as a reason therefor the subterfuge of indisposition. I then repeated the order for him to come on deck and muster the marines. This duty he executed in so careless and indifferent a manner, and at the same time neglected to report to me until called by me and requested so to do, that (conscious that such an occasion ought to animate the most careless and inattentive officer to decision and promptitude) I was induced, from such a manifest neglect of duty, to say to him 'that he might go below, and should do no more duty on board the Java.'

"On the evening of the 18th of September he addressed to me a letter, written by himself, which he caused to be laid on the table in the cabin, and which I received at a very late hour. This letter being couched in language which I deemed indecorous and disrespectful, I sent for him and demanded why he had selected a time so obviously improper. He immediately assumed a manner so highly irritating and contemptuous that I believed it my duty to arrest him (after having expressed to him my indignation at such conduct), and for this purpose sent for the second marine officer, at the same time ordering him to be silent. In utter disregard of this order, though repeatedly warned of the consequences of his disobedience, he persevered in the same irritating tone and manner until at length, after reiterating attempts to effect his silence, I gave him a blow. Frequent outrage added to frequent insult provoked this disagreeable consequence.

"Mortified that I should so far forget myself as to raise my arm against any officer holding a commission in the service of the United States, however improper his conduct might have been and however just the cause, I immediately, in conformity to this principle, offered to make such an apology as should be proper for both. This proposal was refused, which precluded the necessity of any further overtures. The offer was consonant to the views of some of the most distinguished officers of the squadron after their being made fully acquainted with every particular.

"From my having been educated in the strictest discipline of the navy—in which respect and obedience to a superior was instilled into my mind as a fundamental and leading principle—and from a natural disposition to chastise insolence and impertinence immediately when offered me, even in private life, must be inferred the burst of indignant feeling which prompted me to inflict personal satisfaction on an officer who thus daringly outraged the vital interests of the service in my own person.

"I have thus gone through this unpleasant recital with as much candor and conciseness as possible. I might, indeed, detail to you other acts of delinquency in this officer, but I will not further weary you with the circumstances of this unfortunate affair, but confine myself to the request that you will be pleased to order a court of inquiry or court-martial, as you may see fit, to examine into the causes which led to this seeming infraction of the laws of the navy.

"After eighteen years of important and arduous services in the cause of my country, it can hardly be imagined that I have any disposition to infringe that discipline, which is the pride and ornament of the navy; and to prevent any intention being falsely ascribed to me, I beg you will give immediate attention to this quest, that the navy, as well as my country, shall be satisfied of the integrity of my motives.

"I have the honor to be, sir,

"Very respectfully, your obedient servant,

[Signed] "O. H. PERRY.

"To ISAAC CHAUNCEY, Esq., Commodore, etc."

Now it is not the intention here to indulge in explanations or excuses. All we can say is that Perry's conduct after the affair was such as only to increase the love and respect of his countrymen, and can not fail to arouse in our minds to-day the same sentiments. A court-martial censured both officers, and Perry accepted the verdict without comment.

He promptly offered to make an honorable apology to Captain Heath, and submitted this in writing to him; but Heath refused to accept it under any circumstances.

Dueling, unfortunately, was common in those days in almost every branch of military service, and there were few men who escaped at some time during their lives having the disagreeable necessity of looking into the eyes of another man, who may previously have been a friend and comrade, over the notched sights of a pistol.

Heath was bound to call Perry out if such a thing were possible, and he neglected no opportunities to let this fact be known.

Perry had returned to Newport in March, 1817, and there, in connection with Commodore Bainbridge and Captain Evans, he was kept busy for some months surveying the harbor and making arrangements for placing a naval station, depot, and dockyard. In July he had retired from the command of the Java, upon which occasion there was a ceremony that must have touched him deeply, for the officers of the ship presented him with a testimonial of their affection and respect.

Everything went well and happily till the following year, when Captain Heath, who had come over to this country, appeared in Rhode Island, claiming and demanding honorable satisfaction for the injury he had received in the Mediterranean. Perry thought for a long time over the matter, and came at last to the conclusion that, under the code, if Captain Heath would not accept an apology, he was in honor bound to meet him. The State authorities, however, had got wind of the affair, and took steps to intervene and prevent the meeting. So Perry, who was apparently anxious to oblige Captain Heath, even against his own will, agreed to go on to Washington on the 10th of October and give him the satisfaction he wished.

He had written a long letter asking Commodore Decatur to be his second in the affair, and the latter had accepted immediately. Alas, poor Decatur! He was soon to fall before an adversary's bullet in a useless duel, as all duels most probably were.

Before the meeting took place Perry wrote the following letter, had it signed by Decatur and his other friends, and insisted upon Heath's seconds signing it also. It is quoted here *verbatim:*

"Captain Perry desires it to be explicitly understood that, in according to Captain Heath the personal satisfaction he had demanded, he has been influenced by a sense of what he considers due from

him as an atonement to the violated rules of the service, and not by any considerations of the claims which
Captain Heath may have for making such a demand,
which he totally denies, as such claims have been for-
feited by the measures of a public character which
Captain Heath has adopted toward him. If, there-
fore, the civil authority should produce an impossibil-
ity of meeting at the time and place designed, which
he will take every precaution to prevent, he will consider himself absolutely exonerated from any responsibility to Captain Heath touching their present cause
of difference."

One fine fall day—the 19th of October, to be more
exact—a little party of eight persons descended from
two coaches that drove into a wood road that ran
through a little forest on the Jersey shore of the Hudson. Two of the men carried small mahogany boxes,
and when a clearing was reached the errand of the
party was easily seen.

Two of the men strolled off to one side; they
both were young, in the very heyday of manhood.

" I have firmly made up my mind upon this subject," said one, speaking in a low tone of voice. " I
have no animosity toward the fellow at all. It is just
an atonement that I make for an infringement of the
regulations and etiquette of the service."

" Do as you think best," returned the other, " but

it is against my wishes and advice. It is quixotic, and you run great risks. My advice is to wing him."

Suddenly a voice broke in:

"Are you ready, gentlemen?" and then two men faced one another but a short distance apart, pistols hanging in their right hands, for it was agreed at the word "three" they would raise and fire, instead of dropping into the position.

"One, two, three!" counted one of the seconds.

There came but a single shot, and that from Captain Heath's pistol, that was smoking in his hand.

Perry stood there silent and motionless. He was unhurt, and had not moved a finger to lift his weapon. He had made his atonement.

"Are you satisfied?" he asked Captain Heath politely.

"I am, sir," was the captain's return.

Perry handed the unused pistol to one of the seconds, and taking Decatur's arm hastened to one of the carriages. His conduct was just what might have been expected from such a high-hearted and noble-minded man, and that he escaped injury and that a tragedy was averted became reasons for great rejoicing everywhere.

During the year 1819 pirates swarmed and infested the waters of the Caribbean Sea, and Commodore Perry was sent there in the old frigate John Adams, in company with the None Such, in order to put a

stop to the piracy, and to make official visits to the
West Indian governors and to the north shores of
South America.

Yellow fever was rife all along the coast, and while
ashore at Venezuela the young commodore was subject to contagion and contracted the disease. He
was taken aboard his ship, with the fond hope that he
might recover at sea, but on the 23d of August (which,
by the way, was his birthday) he died on shipboard,
just as his vessel was entering the port of Spain on
the island of Trinidad. There he was buried with full
military honors, and seventeen years afterward his
remains were brought back to his native town, and
there they rest under a granite monument on the hill
looking down over the waters.

His example left a deep imprint upon the minds
of his brother officers in the service, and his loss was
mourned by a whole country, and by a devoted wife
and four children who survived him. He was but
thirty-four when he gave up his final command, but
his life had been filled with fine things finely done,
and was rounded to completion at an age when most
men are entering into the fullness of their powers.

THE END.

www.ingramcontent.com/pod-product-compliance
Lightning Source LLC
Chambersburg PA
CBHW030602040726
47497CB00008B/2825